White Jade Tiger

White Jade Tiger

Julie Lawson

DUNDURN
TORONTO

Cover image: © themoderncanvas/ 123RF.com
Printer: Webcom

Revised 2nd edition, first published in 1993

Library and Archives Canada Cataloguing in Publication

Lawson, Julie, 1947-, author
     White jade tiger / Julie Lawson.

     Issued in print and electronic formats.

ISBN 978-1-4597-3755-6 (paperback).--ISBN 978-1-4597-3756-3 (pdf).--
ISBN 978-1-4597-3757-0 (epub)

     I. Title.

PS8573.A94W5 2016   jC813'.54   C2016-906094-2
                                              C2016-906095-0

1   2   3   4   5   20   19   18   17   16

Conseil des Arts du Canada **Canada Council for the Arts** Canadä **ONTARIO ARTS COUNCIL CONSEIL DES ARTS DE L'ONTARIO** an Ontario government agency un organisme du gouvernement de l'Ontario

We acknowledge the support of the **Canada Council for the Arts** and the **Ontario Arts Council** for our publishing program. We also acknowledge the financial support of the **Government of Ontario**, through the **Ontario Book Publishing Tax Credit** and the **Ontario Media Development Corporation**, and the **Government of Canada**.

Care has been taken to trace the ownership of copyright material used in this book. The author and the publisher welcome any information enabling them to rectify any references or credits in subsequent editions.

— *J. Kirk Howard, President*

VISIT US AT

 dundurn.com | @dundurnpress | dundurnpress | dundurnpress

Dundurn
3 Church Street, Suite 500
Toronto, Ontario, Canada
M5E 1M2

For Patrick

Author's Note

White Jade Tiger is a work of fiction for young readers, not a scholarly account. However, it is based on actual events that took place in the Fraser Canyon during the building of the Canadian Pacific Railway from 1880 to 1885. Every attempt has been made to ensure historical accuracy, and if any errors have been made, they are my fault entirely. To aid the flow of the story, the construction schedule of the railway and certain events were moved forward in time. For instance, the riot in Lytton took place in May 1883, not in September 1882, although the events did happen as described. Also, the *Yale Sentinel* article describing the deaths of Chinese workmen was printed in February 1883, not September 1882 as in the story.

Racist terms such as *Chinaman*, *Celestial*, and *John* were commonly used during this time period, by the daily press and politicians as well as by ordinary citizens. These terms are used by some characters in the story, in the context of those times.

Chinese workers subsisted mainly on a diet of rice and ground salmon. Because of a lack of fresh meat and vegetables, they were constantly suffering from vitamin deficiency. Scurvy was widespread, particularly during the winter of 1882–83, and deaths from scurvy continued well into 1883.

The *William Irving* was the largest sternwheeler ever to travel on the Fraser River. The descriptions are accurate, although for the purposes of the story I allowed the *William Irving* to provide through passage from Victoria to Yale.

The long narrow alley that connects Fisgard Street and Pandora Avenue in Victoria was known to the Chinese as Fan Tan Xiang (Fan Tan Alley). Several fan tan gambling clubs operated there during the 1910s. The gambling den that Jasmine enters in 1881 is my invention, although it is possible that such a place did exist in that location. In the 1880s, several opium factories operated in Chinatown. The opium business was legal until 1908.

The class field trip is written from the point of view of young people discovering Victoria's Chinatown for the first time, and responding to certain aspects of Chinese culture. It is not meant to be a definitive description of Chinese culture.

In 1990, Via Rail discontinued its regular passenger run on the *Canadian*, which followed the CPR tracks through the Fraser Canyon. Although there has been some track realignment and most of the bridges have been replaced, much of the original grade is still used by trains carrying freight through the canyon.

About the romantization of the Chinese language. For place names in the present I have used pinyin (e.g., Beijing and Guangdong) since that is the system used today. The early Chinese in North America spoke southern Chinese dialects such as Cantonese or Toisanese. I have therefore used Cantonese for names and common expressions such as *gung hey fat choy*, *Gim Shan*, *lai see* rather than convert these to pinyin. This choice was made largely for convenience — both my own and that of my readers.

The idea for *White Jade Tiger* originally came from a picture I found of a white jade plaque carved in the form of the White Tiger, a mythical animal identified with the West. This amulet is actually from the Han Period (206 BCE–CE 221), although in the story I date it somewhat earlier to the Qin Dynasty (221–206 BCE). From the earliest times, jade was recognized in the Far East as a precious stone endowed with symbolic and magical powers. The magic associated with the white jade tiger in the story, however, is of my own making.

Historical Note

The first Chinese came to British Columbia from California in 1858, drawn by the gold of the Fraser and Cariboo. As early as 1860, taxes against them were being proposed and debated. Anti-Chinese feeling grew steadily throughout the 1860s and 70s, and in 1878 the legislature passed a bill to exclude Chinese from all public works. For politicians seeking election, an anti-Chinese stand was imperative.

However, all British Columbians wanted the railway — the Canadian Pacific Railway that would unite Canada from sea to sea. And if it couldn't be built without the Chinese, then they would grudgingly accept the Chinese.

Thousands of Chinese came to work for the CPR between 1880 and 1885. At the peak of railway construction in the Fraser Canyon, some 8000 Chinese were employed. During the five-year period, an estimated 1,500 died.

Throughout those years and well into the next century, legislation against the Chinese persisted, as did anti-Chinese feeling on the part of many citizens. In spite of such discrimination, the Chinese presence continued to grow, becoming an integral and enriching thread in the fabric of Canadian society.

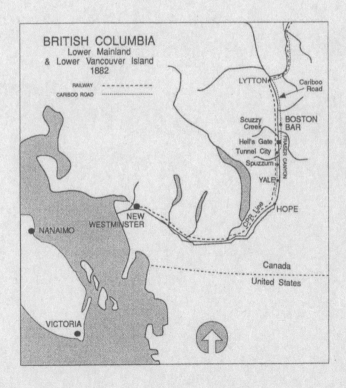

Chapter 1

Jasmine, run! Cords of panic tightened around her chest. Her heart raced with fear.

Run! Don't look back! The warning came too late. Piercing yellow lights sprang out of the blackness. A white shape leaped toward her. She tried to scream but the sound strangled in her throat. Then, total darkness. Pressure. Rising terror. As if she were buried alive.

Run! She struggled to break the paralyzing hold gripping her body. If only she could move, if —

"Aieee!" The scream jolted her awake. For a moment, she didn't know where she was or even who she was. And who had screamed? Surely that hadn't been *her* voice.

For a long time she lay awake, trying to make sense of the recurring nightmare. The voice was becoming clearer. Someone was reaching out to her, and getting closer all the time.

"Two for me, one for the bowl." Jasmine Steele knelt on the damp ground, happily picking her first crop of strawberries. The strawberries had been her project right from the start. "You won't have to do anything," she promised, knowing how her parents hated gardening. "I'll do everything myself." And she had, from buying the plants to keeping out the deer. All her digging, planting, weeding, and watering had resulted in perfect strawberries — plump, juicy, and sweet. *Perfect tens,* she thought, treating herself to another one. *Just like today.*

So what if she'd had the nightmare again. By morning there was never anything left of it, nothing she could remember. And so what if it was raining. The rain brought out the smells of summer — wild roses, freshly cut grass, and the best-ever strawberries. She popped another one into her mouth. Only three weeks until summer holidays, her last summer as a regular kid. In seven months she'd be a teenager. And today, this perfect-ten day, was Thursday. She brushed off her jeans, picked up the bowl, and hummed her way into the house.

"Ta da!" She placed the strawberries on the table, bowed, and with a "Hold the applause!" raced off to the phone.

"Who are you calling?" her mother asked. "Can't it wait till after breakfast?"

"Krista and Becky. I've got to remind them about something."

"You'll be seeing them in ten minutes." With an exasperated sigh, Heather Steele poured herself another cup of coffee. "Just wait," she said to her husband. "As soon as she gets off the phone she'll remind me about tai chi and tell me she'll be late for supper. Every Tuesday and Thursday, for the last six months, she's said the same thing."

Martin Steele laughed. "I'm not going to bet against that one." He bit into a strawberry. "Mmm. These ripened beautifully."

"They wouldn't dare not to," Heather said. "Not with Jasmine growing them."

"What else can we get her to plant this summer? Corn? Peas?" His mouth watered at the thought. "She'd grow a terrific garden."

Heather agreed. "She'll do anything, once she sets her mind to it."

Jasmine bounded back and slid into her chair. "Don't forget, Mom, I've got tai chi after school, so I'll be late for supper." She poured herself a heaping bowl of corn flakes and buried them in strawberries.

"How's Krista? And Becky? Have you got their day organized?"

"Uh-huh. We're practicing our play at recess and lunch. And I reminded them about the hot dog notice. Have you filled mine out?"

"It's in your backpack."

"If you're going shopping we're out of chocolate chip cookies and there's only two apples left." She spread peanut butter on a piece of toast, covered it with slices of apple, then added a layer of strawberries. "Yum! Do you want a bite, Dad?"

"Heavens no," he said. "It looks disgusting."

"You have no taste," she teased. "And don't turn up your nose at something till you've tried it. Ever heard that before?"

"Isn't it time you left for school?"

"Don't worry. Everything's under control." She bolted down the rest of her toast and shoved her lunch and homework inside her backpack. Then she wiped her mouth with the back of her hand, gave her mother and father a peck on the cheek, and raced to the door. "Bye! And don't eat all the strawberries."

"Be careful," her mother called after her. "The roads are slippery."

No problem, Jasmine thought as she tore down the road.

Nothing can go wrong today, not on tai chi Thursday. But what about next month, when the classes were finished?

Well, she'd just have to practice on her own. And there were so many other things she planned to do: swim in the river, camp on the beach, have sleepovers at least once a week, help her mom work on the quilt so it would be finished for her birthday. And this summer, since she was almost thirteen, she was allowed to take the bus into Victoria. She and her friends could go to movies and malls and do all the city things they couldn't do in Sooke. And maybe she'd plant a vegetable garden, since the strawberries were such a success.

"Hey, Krista! Becky!" She spun around the corner to where her friends were waiting. "Is it too late to plant seeds for corn and stuff like that?"

"I don't think so," Krista said. "Why?"

"I've got this great idea for a garden. Do you want to help? We could grow pumpkins too and make a scarecrow...." All the way to school they tossed out ideas, too excited to mind the drizzly rain. By the time they wheeled into the bike racks they had a garden of huge proportions, complete with a goldfish pond and frogs that croaked all night.

"Do you want to come over?" Becky asked, when 3:00 finally came.

"Can't. It's —"

"Tai chi!" Krista looked at Becky and laughed. "You should know by now."

"You should join," Jasmine said. "It's great."

"You should take karate with us."

"No way." Jasmine grinned.

"If we all started, like, tai chi, you'd switch to karate," Becky said. "You're such a nonconformist. Right?"

"Yeah! And proud of it! See you tomorrow — and don't forget about the garden." Jasmine tucked her long black braid inside her hood and headed for her bike. The morning drizzle had turned into a West Coast downpour, making the roads more slippery than ever. Ignoring the puddles, she sped off to her tai chi class.

"Keep your self-control," the teacher was saying. "Don't give in to anger. Remember, tai chi must never be used against another person unless you're in danger. Then, look for a weak spot, maybe the way the person is standing. Take advantage of that weakness. Catch the person off balance."

Jasmine hung onto every word.

"Inner strength is being aware of your own power and energy and having control over it. To have inner strength you must concentrate on your lower stomach, because that's where your power is centred. And remember that tai chi is yin and yang working in harmony. The spiritual side is in balance with the physical side."

As she went through the patterned motions, Jasmine thought about her inner strength. She was sure she had it. She could feel it flowing through her body with every breath.

"Let your arms open as if you're holding the whole world in front of you. Curve your arms downwards and scoop up all this space. Keep your back straight, knees bent. Lift the energy up to your chest."

Jasmine dropped her elbows and rotated her wrists, directing the energy into her lower stomach. She was concentrating so hard she didn't hear the door open or see her teacher walk toward it. She jumped when he tapped her shoulder. "Your dad's here. He wants to talk to you."

She skipped toward the door, eager to show her father the new moves. But the look on his face stopped her abruptly. "Dad? What's —"

"Your mom," he said in a choked voice. He put his arms around her, drawing her close. "There's been an accident."

Somehow, Jasmine left her class, walked down the stairs, and got into the car. "She was driving home," her father was saying. "The roads were slippery, she skidded on a curve, crashed into a tree …" He paused, fighting to control his ragged breathing. "When they got her out she was unconscious but still alive. But she didn't make it to the hospital."

Jasmine stared fixedly through the rain-streaked windshield, barely hearing her father's words. They fluttered through some distant part of her consciousness like fragments of paper, ripped apart, swept away. What was he talking about? Her mother, dead? No! It was a mistake! She wanted to scream, shout, smash — pound everything back into place, the way it had been.

"It can't be," she repeated numbly. Her body throbbed with an overwhelming hurt. She was out of her depth, sinking slowly, with nothing to hold onto, no hope of touching bottom, not even a shred of inner strength to keep her afloat.

And that night, the dreams began.

Chapter 2

Bright Jade sat alone by the pool, staring at the moon's reflection. She tried to capture the image of the Moon Lady, but the wind kept stirring the water, breaking the reflection into ripples.

She looked up at the sky, where the moon hung like a silver coin. Although she still couldn't see the Moon Lady, she could see the hare, pounding out the elixir of immortality at the foot of a cassia tree.

Bright Jade sighed. Everlasting life! How could one attain it? The moon was so far away, yet here it was at her feet — a clear reflection now, not distorted by the wind. If she could just reach over, fall into the pool and land on the moon....

She knew the time was coming, even though the Emperor believed his reign would last ten thousand years.

The mighty Emperor, she thought bitterly. Qin Shi Huangdi, the Son of Heaven, so obsessed with eternal life he sent six thousand boys and girls to the Eastern Sea to search for the Islands of the Immortals. Did they find the magical islands? Or the elixir that was said to grow there? No one knew, for the children were never seen or heard from again.

Then there were the thousands buried beneath the stones of the Great Wall. Young men and old, brothers, husbands, fathers, and sons whose sweat was mixed with the mortar that held the stones together; dead men denied a proper burial, whose souls were doomed to an eternity without rest; dead men whose bones were part of the Great Wall itself, the longest graveyard in the world.

Bright Jade shivered. She was the Emperor's favourite. All the more reason he would insist she accompany him to the Celestial Kingdom, where he would continue to reign long after his body was dead.

The thought of that kingdom made her shudder. Hundreds of thousands of peasants had laboured a lifetime, creating a universe deep within the earth, a universe complete with rivers and ocean, moon and stars. Inside this world lay the burial chamber where the Emperor would rule, surrounded by his treasures: jewels, gold, jade, and the beautiful women who entertained him.

To protect this Celestial Kingdom, the Emperor had created an army of life-size terracotta warriors. Thousands of archers, charioteers, infantry, generals, all clothed in armour, all heavily armed, keeping watch in the huge underground vaults that surrounded the Emperor's tomb.

Bright Jade knew that traps had been placed inside the tomb, intricately set and cunningly concealed. Crossbows were set to shoot anyone who entered. And once the tomb was closed, all the artisans who knew its secrets would be walled up inside, their lips sealed forever. She knew the time was coming.

The moon floated on the black water of the pool, undisturbed by ripples. Bright Jade leaned over. But no sooner had she touched the surface of the water than the moon dissolved into fractures of silvery light, scattering over the pool like broken dreams.

It was then she felt the eyes watching her. Turning slowly, she saw the figure framed by the moon gate. The Old One.

Jasmine woke with a start. Who was this person in her dream? She *knew* her — her thoughts and feelings and memories. But how? And where had the dream come from? The Great Wall was in China, but what connection did she have with China, apart from tai chi?

Suddenly, she saw her mother, waving goodbye. "Be careful, it's slippery…."

Struggling to shut out the pain, she willed herself back to the dream. It was the only way of forgetting. The only sanctuary, in spite of the shadowy figure that lurked there.

Startled, Bright Jade began to rise.

"Do not be frightened," the Old One whispered as he glided toward her. His long frayed robe hung loosely from his shoulders, and the amulets swinging from his neck and waist clattered and tinkled — skulls of small animals, stones and bones; pieces of jade and tiny bronze bells; the shell of a tortoise, the claws of a tiger. "You know me as the gardener," he said. "And I know you, Bright Jade."

She nodded. She had seen him feeding the carp, tending the peach trees. In all weathers he had drifted in and out of the garden, his amulets clattering softly. A mysterious man, the Old One. Some feared him as a sorcerer. Others sought him as a gifted fortune teller. Some had heard him weaving magic spells and chanting incantations. It was said the Emperor himself had consulted him on the question of immortality. But Bright Jade knew him simply as the gardener, an old man with a warm smile and penetrating eyes.

She searched those eyes now, wondering what had brought him out so late at night. And how long had he been watching her?

"Long enough to know you seek the elixir of life," he said, answering her unspoken question.

Bright Jade blushed. "I am foolish to think such thoughts."

"But you think them all the same." The Old One smiled. "And why not? Everyone desires eternal life. You shall have it — though not in the way you imagine. And not in this time or place."

He handed her a small bag. "The time is coming. Inside you will find a jade amulet, hanging on a leather thong. Its magic will protect you in this life and the next. Wear it close to your heart and do not let it leave your possession. For in the hands of another it will bring a curse — to him and to his children and to his children's children. And it will not end until the white jade tiger sleeps again."

Bright Jade took the amulet from the bag. It was carved in the shape of a tiger — watchful, ready to spring. The jade was white, almost translucent. In her hands it shimmered like moonlight.

"Why are you giving it to me?" she asked, placing it around her neck.

"There is a light in you," he said. "A light that will shine far."

She frowned, not understanding. "And the tiger, how will it protect me?"

"You will know when the time comes." Without another word, he slipped away.

Now the time had come. Bright Jade and the others were ordered to accompany the dead Emperor into the tomb. One by one they stepped down the ramp beneath the earth, through the vault of warriors.

Bright Jade passed between the long lines of archers and infantry, feeling their eyes upon her, eyes so lifelike she could almost read their secrets. She trembled at the force carved within them, feeling at any moment they might spring into action, like the tiger she wore next to her heart.

They reached the end of the vault and began to enter the Celestial Kingdom, where the Emperor would reign forever. Bright Jade paused to adjust a hairpin, while the others slipped by in a kaleidoscope of brilliant silks and brocades. As the last one passed, Bright Jade reached inside her gown and clasped the amulet.

A mist swirled up from the depths of the earth, shrouding her in a pale purple haze. She felt herself rising, rising … until she could feel no more.

Somehow, time passed. It wilted through the summer, rustled through autumn, and stormed into January, bringing snow for Jasmine's thirteenth birthday.

"You've been looking forward to this for ages," her father said. "You're sure you don't want a party?"

"Positive. All I want is —" She paused. "There's nothing I really want." *Except to feel whole again.*

The dreams helped, even when they came in puzzling bits and pieces mixed with fragments of the nightmare. For the most part, they unfolded as they had in the beginning — clear and luminous. She felt strangely drawn to Bright Jade, and when the dreams came, she welcomed them as a refuge.

Chapter 3

"Lasagna!" Jasmine smelled it the moment she opened the door. She raced into the kitchen and took a deep breath. The delicious aromas of meat, garlic, tomato sauce, and mozzarella melted through her whole being. "Just the way I like it, with a dash of cinnamon, right?"

Martin grinned. "Right you are. I certainly have you well trained."

Jasmine bit into a slice of French bread, still warm from the oven. "Crusty on the outside — a perfect ten for that, Dad." She popped the rest into her mouth, closing her eyes to savour the taste. "Mmm! That tastes like more."

"Not till you've set the table. I remember training you for that, too."

"Okay, okay. I think this calls for candles. Can I get them?"

"Sure. Get the red ones. They're in the dining room, top drawer of the hutch."

Jasmine hummed as she opened the drawer and took out the candles. As she was reaching for the candlesticks she noticed a shiny folder with the words *Pacific Travel*. She raised the flap and peered inside. Plane tickets! And a sheet of white paper with *Itinerary* printed across the top. Dates, times — Vancouver, Shanghai, Beijing — weren't those places in China? Airlines, luggage information —

"Dinner's served. Have you got the candles?"

"Coming." She closed the drawer, her mind spinning. *We're going on a trip. That's why we're having such a great dinner. He's going to make an announcement about our summer holidays — wait a minute.* She stopped abruptly, holding a burning match in her hand. The dates she had seen were in February. "Ow!"

"Need a hand?" Martin struck a new match and lit the candles. "Please be seated, my dear," he said formally.

"Thank you, kind sir," she replied automatically. French bread, her father's specialty. Lasagna with spinach noodles, her favourite. Tossed green salad with homemade dressing. And for dessert — "Dad, did you by any chance make raspberry mousse?" Raspberry mousse was her all-time favourite, served only on special occasions.

"Jasmine," he said, smiling, "you know me too well."

"Just a lucky guess." She did know him well. Well enough to know he had something up his sleeve. Raspberry mousse and lasagna on a weeknight in February? The last time they'd had such a feast was a month ago, on her birthday. There was a reason for all this, and seeing that travel folder clinched it. Still, she'd play along for a while and let him tell her in his own way, in his own time.

"How was school today?" he asked.

Jasmine swallowed another mouthful of lasagna. "Best ever," she said. "The lasagna, I mean. But school was okay too. We're learning about China. Did you know that nearly one out of every four people in the world lives in China? And we're doing shadow puppet plays about Chinese folktales. My group is doing a story about a dragon and I'm making all the scenery — the river and a pagoda and rainclouds, and we just cut the stuff out of paper and for colour we put in cellophane so the light shines through —"

"Hold it!" Her father laughed. "Once you get going, there's no stopping you. Don't let your dinner get cold. Here, have some more bread."

"Thanks," she said, taking her fourth piece. "But you were the one who asked."

"Fair enough," he said.

They ate in silence for a while, enjoying the meal. Now and then Jasmine looked up and caught his eye. He winked and smiled.

"You're like Mrs. Butler," she said.

"How's that? Does she have a moustache like mine?"

"No, silly. She always winks."

"Oh, I see."

"I like it when she winks. But you're much better at it. And you've been doing it more often lately."

"Why's that, I wonder."

Jasmine gave him a knowing look, but he took another helping of lasagna and kept on eating. She tried a different approach. "My class is going to Victoria on Friday, to Chinatown. And we're having lunch in a Chinese restaurant."

"What a great idea! To celebrate Chinese New Year?"

Jasmine nodded. "It's the Year of the Snake. And after lunch we can look around the shops and buy souvenirs. So can I have some money, please?"

"I knew it. How much?"

"Four dollars for lunch."

"A bargain."

"Mrs. Butler got a special deal."

"And you want some souvenir money?"

"No, it's okay. I've got lots in my piggy bank."

"Maybe I'll borrow some from you."

"For your trip, you mean?" There. It was out.

His mouth fell open in surprise. "How did you know about that? I was going to tell you tonight."

"I just happened to see the travel folder in the drawer. You're not very good at hiding things, Dad. Anyway, I was wondering why we're having such a special dinner. I mean, it's a rainy Wednesday in February and it's nobody's birthday. So why the celebration?"

"How about some dessert?" he asked, removing the plates.

"Don't change the subject! Where are we going? And when?" She carried the bowls of mousse to the table. "I saw the word February on your itin-whatever, but there must be some mistake because we can't go anywhere in February." She took a heaping spoonful of the mousse and let it sit on her tongue before swallowing. "Mmm," she sighed. "Best ever, Dad. But what were those places again? I thought the ticket said Shanghai and Beijing — that's the capital, isn't it? But come on, we're not seriously going to China! And why, Dad? Why China?"

"Whew!" Her father wiped his brow. "She's finally stopped talking." He put down his spoon and looked at her with an unusually serious expression. "Jasmine."

An uneasy feeling crept over her.

"The thing is … I'm going to China alone. I've accepted a job at a college in Beijing. The professor who was there got sick and had to come home. So I'm going to take her place. I'll be leaving on Friday."

"*This* Friday?" Jasmine exploded. "That's only two days away! That's impossible! You can't! You never asked, you never told me — and where am I going to go? Why didn't you tell me?" She pushed the bowl of unfinished mousse across the table, hoping it would fall in his lap or crash in a mess on the floor.

He reached out his hand and stopped it. "I understand you're upset and hurt and angry. But I'd like you to listen while I explain. Can you do that?"

She turned away. Nothing seemed real. Dishes piled on the counter, pictures on the wall, magnets on the fridge — everything was a piece of some other life, totally unconnected to her own. Even her father's voice sounded distant, as if he had already gone away.

"This has been a difficult time for both of us, since your mother's death. At first I thought I'd made the right decision, taking a year off. And for a while, it *was* the right decision. I've enjoyed being home, being here for you, writing my book, cooking up a storm now and then." He winked, but she didn't respond. "It's not enough, though. Jasmine, you can't begin to imagine how much I miss your mother."

What about me? The feeling of helplessness raged inside. She felt it would eat her away, one piece at a time, until there was nothing left.

"So after Christmas I went to the university and said I'd take any opening that came along. Naturally, I thought I'd get something in Victoria. But when this Beijing position turned up, I couldn't say no. Besides, I've always wanted to go to China."

Jasmine glared. *China?* He'd never told her that. They were so close, she thought she knew everything about him.

"They're expecting me by the middle of February. So I'm leaving tomorrow night for Vancouver and flying to China early Friday morning. I'll get settled and send for you as soon as I can. Meanwhile, you'll be staying with Val in Victoria. She said she'd drive you to Sooke, even though it's a long way, so you won't have to change schools."

Jasmine was too stunned to speak.

"If you don't want to come to China, you can stay with her until I get back. My contract goes till the end of June, so I'll be home sometime after that."

"Auntie Val?" She spat out the words. "You seriously expect me to stay with her? How *could* you? I hardly even know her! And I suppose it's already arranged. You did all this behind my back!" She leaped from her chair, wanting to hit him. "Wait a minute! You're always wanting to go to Victoria, and you like Val — why this sudden change? She lives in a fantastic apartment overlooking the harbour, two steps from Chinatown. You'll love it."

"No, I won't love it! Don't you dare take off to the other side of the world and tell me I'll *love* it! I'll *hate* it! And I hate you!"

Choking back the tears, she kicked over the chair and fled to her room, slamming the door behind her.

Chapter 4

The storyteller shuffled from village to village, shoulders hunched under the weight of the baskets slung on his bamboo pole. With any luck he wouldn't have to dip into his meagre rations, for the villagers were usually willing to share their rice in return for a story or two. But in this Year of the Snake times were hard, and people barely had enough food for themselves let alone a wandering storyteller.

The man sighed. For many years now, times had been hard in the farming districts of southern China. Too many people, too little food. And the gods had not been kind. If it wasn't a flood, it was a drought. If not a plague, then a famine. If that weren't enough, local wars between clans had erupted and set bandits loose upon the countryside.

He remembered the day his village had been overrun by bandits. He had returned from the hills to find the whole village in ashes and the starving peasants killed, including his own family.

Now he trudged throughout the countryside, seeking refuge in his stories. What else was there? Farming was impossible; he had no money to rent a field and no hope of ever paying back a loan. Become a pirate? A soldier? No, he was too old. And far too old to move to the land across the sea as so many others were doing. He shuddered at the thought. He might starve or meet a violent death, but at least his bones would be buried in his homeland. What more could a man hope for?

Some kindness from the gods, he thought, answering his own question. *Too long, the gods have been angry. Perhaps if the right offering were made, or if the curse were broken....*

His senses quivered suddenly, as a willow wand dips when it discovers water. Could this be the place? It wasn't often that he thought of the curse but when he did, he felt a pull, sometimes weak, sometimes strong, but never as strong as this. Every nerve tingled. This was the place.

A bright chattering interrupted his thoughts. Young voices cascaded through the village and rice paddies, announcing his arrival. "The storyteller is coming!" Before he knew it, he was surrounded by villagers of all ages.

Chan Tai Keung rushed along with the others, glad of the distraction. Perhaps this would set his uneasy mind at rest. Besides, who knew when the opportunity would come again?

"Tell us, Elder Uncle," the children clamoured. "Tell us a story."

He settled himself beneath a shady tree. "First I need my story bag," he said. From one of his baskets he took a tattered pouch. He reached in, gathered a handful of yellow sand, and flung it high into the air. The grains fell like a sprinkling of gold dust. He caught a grain on the tip of his finger and looked at it for a moment, lost in thought. Then he said, "This is the story that wants to be told. Two thousand years ago, there lived a Mighty Emperor who built the Great Wall of China …"

Keung tried to concentrate on the words but could not. Besides, he knew the story of the Emperor and the Wall. And he knew about the great tomb and the army of warriors built to protect the Emperor after his death.

His mind drifted away from the wrinkled face of the storyteller, far away to *Gim Shan,* the Land of Gold Mountain across the sea. There he would make his fortune. He would buy enough food for everyone. Never again would the villagers be forced to eat boiled grass or suck on stones to still the pangs of hunger.

The streets of Gold Mountain would be paved with gold. His pockets would be lined with gold dust, bright as the yellow sand scattered at his feet. And he would not return alone, but with his father.

"… dreams turn to dust." The storyteller's voice drew him back. "Until the white jade tiger sleeps again."

The storyteller took a long draw from his pipe and exhaled. In the curling smoke, Keung imagined a fierce tiger leaping through the air.

"Just before Bright Jade entered the tomb," the storyteller continued, "she clutched the amulet. A mist appeared, wrapped her like a silkworm in a cocoon, and swept her away from the darkness, into the light. Far away to the south, to a land of lush green and sunshine, where she married a hard-working farmer and lived to have many sons and grandsons."

His eyes twinkled as he scanned the villagers. They knew this story. Since they belonged to the same clan, they shared the same ancestors, all the way back to Bright Jade.

He lowered his voice. "Bright Jade was not an ordinary woman. She had mysterious powers and seemed to be unaffected by such things as heat or cold, discomfort or pain, almost as if she were a spirit and not a real person. Many believed the village prospered because of her protection, or because of her amulet, the white jade tiger. It was believed this amulet gave her immortality as well as other powers, for Bright Jade lived on and on. But the day finally came when she passed to the other life. And when she was buried, the white jade tiger went with her. Her spirit was at peace and continued to watch over her clan.

"But many years ago, the rains came with a vengeance. The land was flooded with the rising waters of the river. Many graves were disturbed. From one such grave, the white jade tiger was awakened. And lost."

The storyteller held the villagers with his gaze. "What has become of it? Was it swept away by the river? Buried deep in the mud? Or was it stolen to satisfy a longing for riches?

"Bright Jade is restless. In dreams she appears, calling for it. Through time and space she wanders, searching for it." The storyteller rested his eyes on Keung. "The clan of Bright Jade will have no peace until the tiger is found."

Keung trudged toward the mountain looming in his dream. In the shadow of the mountain a tall, slender girl appeared, braiding her long black hair. Although he could not see her face clearly, he sensed that she was smiling. Encouraged, he quickened his pace. "Embrace the mountain," she was saying. "Return the white jade tiger." Keung frowned, puzzled. What did she mean?

A cold wind slashed his face. It scattered the girl's words and swept her straight into the mountain. "Wait," he cried, stumbling after her. Then he was falling, falling over rocks and gravel in a headlong rush to the muddy river below.

"Aiee!" he screamed as he hit the water. He struggled to remain above the surface, but the whirling eddies sucked him down. Another scream woke him and he sat up gasping for air, his thoughts spinning. The land must be Gold Mountain. But who was the girl? Bright Jade? Of course! Her spirit had found the tiger and was urging him to bring it home.

But how did it get to Gold Mountain? And how would he ever find it?

Keung wore a brave face the next morning, hoping it would hide his nervousness.

"It is cold across the sea," his mother said as she helped pack his bag. "You must take warm clothing and shoes with thick soles." She handed him some packages. "Special herbs, in case you get sick. They will not have such good medicines in *Gim Shan*."

Keung felt a prickling behind his eyes, but knew it was bad luck to cry. Carefully, he tucked the packages inside his cotton bag.

"And take the letter. It may help you find your father."

Keung took the worn envelope and remembered how eagerly he and his mother had rushed to the nearest town to have it read. She had made the letter-writer read it over and over so that every word would stay fixed in her mind. Three long years ago.

"Don't worry, Mother," he said. "I'll find Father and we'll be home before you know it."

Keung was not the only one leaving the district, although at fifteen he was the youngest. They smiled and talked about the land they would buy when they returned, but their hearts lurched painfully, knowing they were leaving their families to untold hardships. The crop was a poor one, even worse than the one before. Almost every family would have to borrow from the moneylender to pay the landlord. Only those receiving money from relatives in *Gim Shan* would be free from debt.

Like the others, Keung had heard stories about the opportunities in *Gim Shan*. Railway workers made a fortune! After five years or so, enough money could be made to return and live comfortably for a lifetime.

The thoughts clattered through his mind like the clacking of buttons in a game of fan tan. But like fan tan, it was a gamble. Keung couldn't help but worry. His travelling companions had signed a contract to work on the new railway; he alone was staying in the Big Port called Victoria, where his father had last been heard from. And now, not only must he find his father, but also a jade tiger, small enough to hold in the palm of his hand.

He thought about the curse as he strode along with the others. Drought, floods, famine, wars — they could not be blamed on one amulet, surely. The whole district was affected by such disasters. But within his family, three younger sisters had died as babies. His brother had drowned in the river, leaving Keung the only son. Two uncles were killed by bandits — why, every family in his clan had suffered some misfortune or other. And now his father was lost in the Land of Gold Mountain.

He walked a little taller as he realized how important he would feel, once the tiger was returned to its proper place. Then, quickly, he pushed the thought from his mind. The gods must not think him too bold. It would not be wise to anger them before he even reached Gold Mountain.

Chapter 5

For the first time in her life, Jasmine hated every second of the forty-five-minute drive to Victoria. She maintained a stony silence, nurturing the hostility she felt toward her father. For a while he rambled on about China, and how they could explore it together when she flew out to join him — but only if she wanted to, he added hastily. Then he switched to questions: had she packed everything, had she remembered the pieces for her quilt, was there anything she needed, anything she wanted…? She continued to ignore him. Finally he stopped talking and turned on the radio. For once, Jasmine didn't complain about his choice of stations.

They travelled along the winding road, past the rush hour traffic inching through the suburbs, onto the highway. Past service stations, used car lots, sprawling shopping centres. Flashing lights, howling sirens, screeching brakes. Jasmine winced. Why had she ever wanted to take the bus into Victoria? *'Cause it would have been* fun, her inner voice said. Fun, with her friends. Not like now. Not like getting dumped by her father.

"Do you want to do any shopping?" he asked. "We could stop at a mall."

Silence.

"Well, we are stopping for supper. Any requests?"

Jasmine shrugged. When he pulled into her favourite fast food restaurant she refused to show the slightest interest.

"What? No cheeseburger? Milkshake? You've got to eat something."

She shook her head and picked at the fries and onion rings.

After supper they crept along Douglas Street, crowded with pedestrians and traffic. People swept in and out of stores and restaurants, hurrying to finish their shopping or grab a bite before heading home.

"Thought we'd go through Chinatown," her father said, "since you're going there tomorrow."

An Oriental gate arched across Fisgard Street, shining an invitation to enter. As they drove down the block, Jasmine felt her pulse quicken, stirred by the lights, colour, movement, and sound. But she remained silent.

Soon they were crossing the Johnson Street Bridge, the lift bridge that was raised whenever boats passed through the Inner Harbour. Her father made his usual remark about its odd shade of blue, but Jasmine did not respond. Finally, they were turning into the parking lot of Val's condominium. "Straight up to the ninth floor," he said.

"My lucky number," Jasmine muttered. "Some luck." They stepped out of the elevator and walked down the hallway to 927. "The door number even adds up to nine," her father said. "Eighteen, actually, but add those two digits and you get nine. What do you think of that?"

Val was waiting at the door. "Hi, Martin," she said, giving him a hug. "Come on in. Jasmine! Welcome to the double lucky condo. Pretty auspicious, don't you think?"

"Auspicious?" Great. She couldn't even understand her aunt's language.

"Favourable. A good omen. Nine's my lucky number, you see. And you were born in the Year of the Dragon, weren't you? A very lucky sign. But I could go on and on about auspicious symbols. Martin, how about some coffee?" As she was talking, Val bustled about the kitchen, setting up the coffee maker, slicing Nanaimo bars, arranging butter tarts on plates. "Jasmine, you probably feel a bit strange about being here, so why don't I show you your room and you can get settled." She caught her eyeing the Nanaimo bars and laughed. "Don't worry, we'll save you some."

Jasmine followed her down the hall. "Here you are. Fill up the drawers and closet with your things. Read any of the books you want. Enjoy the view."

"Wow!" The exclamation slipped out, in spite of Jasmine's vow to be miserable.

The scene was magical, so different from home where there wasn't even a streetlight. Across the Inner Harbour, the Legislative Buildings shimmered like a fairyland. The posh Empress Hotel, where her mother had once taken her for tea, glowed like a castle, with lights shining from its turrets. The streets were lit with round white globes set on old-fashioned lampposts. Lights from boats were reflected in the water, and lights from high-rises shone across the harbour. She couldn't deny it. The view was a perfect ten.

"Help yourself," Val said when she returned to the kitchen. "Here's a glass of milk."

"Thanks. It's a great view."

Her father beamed. "What did I tell you?"

"Good Nanaimo bars." Jasmine smiled at her aunt and pointedly ignored him.

"Well," he said after an awkward silence. "I've got to rush off. Anything you want to say before I go?"

Jasmine took a butter tart and remained silent. *Don't look at him,* she told herself firmly. *Look at him and you'll start to cry. So don't look.* She tried to swallow but the pastry stuck in her throat.

What's he waiting for? she wondered. *Why doesn't he just go?*

After another awkward silence, he said, "Good luck then, honey." He leaned over to kiss her cheek and gently wiped the tear that was starting to fall. "I'll phone when I arrive and write two minutes later. Thanks for everything, Val. Take care."

Then he was gone.

"Can I work on my quilt?" Jasmine asked.

Her aunt looked surprised. "There's nothing on TV you want to watch? No homework?"

Jasmine shook her head.

"There's a sewing machine in the spare room," Val said. "Let me know if you need anything."

Within minutes, Jasmine had set up her cutting board and emptied the bag of scraps. "A memory quilt," her mother had said when she started the project. "Every bit of fabric will remind you of something, a time or a place or a person. With any luck I'll have it finished for your birthday."

"Can I help?" Jasmine had asked.

"Of course! Here, sort these pieces into lights and darks."

Later, her mother showed her how to cut four triangles at once. Before long there were hundreds of triangles, from pale blues to deep forest greens, from flowery pastels to wild fluorescent pinks. "Is this enough?" Jasmine had asked.

Her mother laughed. "This quilt has to cover your bed, you know. We're not even half done."

Two months later, they'd celebrated the halfway mark by drinking raspberry ginger ale and listening to the summer rain. That was the night before the accident.

"That's all she wants to do, Val." Surrounded by fabric scraps in her aunt's spare room, Jasmine remembered what her father had said the night before. The phone was down the hall and he was trying to speak softly, but she could hear every word. "Since Heather's death she's lost interest in everything, even tai chi. Never sees her friends, except at school. Just stays in her room, reads or works on her quilt. Maybe a change of scenery would help…. She's always been independent, but now she's so reclusive…." On and on and on. Analyzing her. Arranging her life.

She stroked her cheek with a piece of red velvet, remembering her first special Christmas dress. A flash of metallic silver brought back a wizard's cape and a Halloween party. "That's all she wants to do." It was true. She felt safe, leafing through the fragments of her past. As if putting the pieces together would bring back something that was gone, and make her feel whole again. Even though the configuration could never be the same.

Lights and darks, like the yin and yang she learned about in tai chi class. Yin — earth, female, moon, darkness. Yang — heaven, male, sun, light. Together, a balance in the universe. Harmony.

Triangles into squares, small squares into larger squares. Fitting together to make a whole. Everything ordered, the way it was supposed to be. Clean, straight lines. Clear, sharp edges. Perfect points. *Mom would be pleased it's getting finished*, she thought. *Pleased that we're almost there.*

When Val came to say good night, Jasmine remembered.

"We're going on a field trip to Chinatown tomorrow, so I'll meet my class there and you won't have to drive me to school. Did Dad tell you?"

Her aunt nodded. "I'll drop you off at eleven."

"We can wear something Chinese if we like, but I don't have anything."

Val grinned. "I've got just the thing."

In a minute she was back holding a dark bundle and a wide-brimmed hat. "What do you think?" she asked, placing the hat on Jasmine's head.

Jasmine looked in the mirror. "Great!"

"Now this." She held a jacket against Jasmine's chest. "Looks like it might even fit. Try it on."

The jacket was lined inside, heavily padded with cotton. It had wide sleeves and hung loosely over her jeans. Jasmine did up the frog fastenings, closing herself in from neck to hem. "It fits perfectly."

"It's what the Chinese coolies wore when they came to work on the railway. Try on the pants."

Jasmine slipped them on. "A bit long."

"That's okay. We'll just roll them up, like so. Now, the shoes." She handed her a pair of black cotton shoes.

"These fit too."

Val smiled. "You've certainly got the hair for it. One long pigtail, like the Chinese had in those days."

The clothes felt well-worn and comfortable. Jasmine grinned at her reflection. "I look just like a Chinese coolie."

Val's face fell.

"What's wrong?" Jasmine asked, surprised at her aunt's reaction.

"Nothing," Val said, laughing it off. "It's the way you looked just then. Have you ever had the feeling that something has happened before? *Déjà vu,* it's called. When your mom was about your age, she went to a Halloween party. She didn't know what to wear, so I suggested the coolie clothes. She put them on, stood in front of the mirror and said exactly what you said."

"Did she wear them to the party?"

"Yes, and had a horrible time. The kids teased her and called her names. She came home in tears, tore off the clothes and kicked them out of the room. This is the first time they've been worn since then." Seeing the look on Jasmine's face, she added, "Don't worry. I'm sure the kids in your class are more enlightened."

For a long time Jasmine couldn't sleep. Night sounds hummed outside the window, and in spite of the closed curtains, city light crept in. She buried her face in the pillow, willing her mind to bring Bright Jade and the sanctuary of the garden.

But this time, there was no garden. The dream was a ragbag of images. Mist rising above a swollen river, like a dragon's breath. Flood waters, flashes of white. Bright Jade, weeping. And mud! Grains of yellow sand, turning to mud. The claws of a tiger, sinking in mud. A river, churning with mud. Then turning to waves, blue-black and clear, whipped into spray by the wind.

A ship, crowded with hundreds of bodies. A boy about her age, standing alone, head bowed, sick with anxiety. All of a sudden he looked up and locked his gaze with hers. For one brief moment she felt a tug, as if some force was trying to pull her in.

She moaned, reeling with the lurching motion of the ship, nauseated by the stench that permeated the quarters. She woke with a start, certain she was going to be sick.

The instant she opened her eyes she felt better. Too many Nanaimo bars? Or just muddled thinking? She groaned at the pun, rolled over, and tried to get back to sleep.

But the assortment of images would not go away. Like her scraps of fabric, they were fragments of light and dark. Somehow they were related. Somehow they fit together. If only she could discover how.

Chapter 6

Keung scanned the coast with dismay as the ship slid along the grey-green shoreline of Vancouver Island. There were no gold mountains, nothing but dark forests. No sign of gold at all, except for a sliver of sunlight shining through a break in the clouds.

He shivered. In spite of his fifteen years, he felt terribly young and afraid. Some Tiger Boy. Those born in the Year of the Tiger were supposed to be courageous and powerful. He hoped his ancestors could not see this far to the west. They would be ashamed.

He stared at his surroundings as the ship was towed into Victoria's Inner Harbour. Past the Legislative Buildings with their pagoda-like appearance, past a long wooden bridge that crossed a bay and mudflats. Sailing ships and paddlewheelers jammed the harbour. A brick building sat high on the waterfront, overlooking the docks and a forest of masts and rigging. Wharves, boathouses, sheds, and warehouses stood along the shore, dotted with rowboats and canoes. Lining the harbour were boardwalks and dirt roads, crowded with horse-drawn carriages and men on horseback.

How dismal it was, this place they called Victoria. Where was the warmth? "They want us to come," he had been told. "They will make us welcome."

As he made his way from the wharf to the street, he knew it wasn't true. He wasn't wanted. White people on the boardwalk stared at him with loathing. He couldn't dismiss them as "foreign devils," barbarians that aroused one's curiosity, for now *he* was the foreigner, the unwelcome stranger in their midst.

Two white youths shouldered past, pushing him into the dusty road. Insults were hurled at him, ugly words he had first heard from the sailors on the ship.

What was it his mother had said? "The stranger must be invisible." If only it were so. He had never felt so vulnerable or alone.

Those who had signed on as labourers for the new railway were already on their way to construction camps in the Fraser Canyon. For now, his job was to find his father. Then he would work on the railway and make enough money for them to return home, away from this chilling place. Although that would mean another long sea voyage.

He shuddered at the thought. As the ship was sailing out of Hong Kong, he and the others had tossed grains of rice into the water so that the gods would give them a safe voyage. And safe it was — at least they hadn't been shipwrecked. But how awful! Five weeks below deck, hundreds of them packed into cramped quarters, often with the hatches closed. Every two days they were allowed on deck for a few moments of fresh air and exercise while their quarters were cleaned. Everyone was seasick. And the food! Very little rice, no fresh fruit or vegetables.

"Aiee!" he cried, as a stone hit the back of his head. He turned to see a group of boys laughing and jeering. Another stone hit him in the arm.

Keung's face burned with humiliation. The shakiness in his legs made it difficult to stride with confidence, but he straightened his shoulders and quickened his pace, hoping he looked braver than he felt. The taunting voices followed, and echoed in his mind long after the boys had gone.

Gradually, Keung became aware of changes. Buildings of brick and stone gave way to a jumble of wooden shacks. The number of white people lessened, and the sound of his own dialect filtering through open doorways lifted his spirits. Feeling more confident, he approached a group of Chinese men chatting on the corner. "Elder Uncles," he said, "I've just come off the ship. My name is Chan Tai Keung and I'm looking for the one they call Dragon Maker."

They clustered around him, eager for news from their homeland. Finally one of the men said, "Leave him be. Can't you see how tired he is? Come, boy. I'll take you to Dragon Maker. But are you sure that's where you want to go?"

Keung took out the letter. "Dragon Maker wrote this for my father, three years ago."

As the man read the letter, his brow creased and the scar on his cheek seemed to twitch. "Chan Sam is your father?" he asked. "And this was the last you heard from him?"

"Yes," said Keung. "Do you know him?"

The man shrugged. "Perhaps. So many come and go."

"He came to make money so we could buy our land," Keung said. "My mother's afraid something has happened, since he hasn't written for so long. It was decided I should come and find him. And I must find —" A look on the man's face made him stop short of mentioning the white jade tiger.

"Go on, what must you find?"

Keung grinned sheepishly. "Only my fortune."

"Do you have money?"

"No, all our money went for my passage. But I'll make money."

"It may not be so easy." The man paused. "You could work for me."

"For you?"

"I'm Blue-Scar Wong, a merchant in Chinatown. I own some shops and a restaurant."

Keung was amazed. So it was true! One could come to this strange land and make a fortune. Gratefully, he accepted the merchant's offer.

They walked along a narrow alley and entered a warren of ramshackle shanties, thrown together with lumber of all shapes and sizes. Two or three were piled on top of each other, with rotting steps leading to the upper floors. Blue-Scar Wong led the way up a steep staircase and knocked on a faded red door, the only door that was painted. "Dragon Maker, you have a visitor," he called loudly. "It's Chan Tai Keung, looking for his father."

The door opened a crack. Two bright eyes peered out.

"That's Dragon Maker," said Blue-Scar. "He'll let you stay here for the night. Tomorrow morning you start working for me. Tomorrow you start making your fortune." Chuckling softly, he descended the rickety stairs.

"Wait! I have to —" Keung began, but Blue-Scar was already out of sight.

"Never mind, Chan Tai Keung."

He turned at the sound of the voice. An old man stood in the doorway, a slow smile spreading across his face. "I am Dragon Maker," he said. "Come inside."

Keung gasped as he entered the tiny room. Painted dragons stared at him from every corner and every shelf. A table stood in the centre, covered with dragons in various stages of completion. Jars of brushes and pots of glaze spilled over the table in splashes of red, yellow, blue, and green.

"Tea?" Dragon Maker cleared a spot on the table and filled two chipped cups.

"Please." Keung slipped the bamboo pole off his shoulder and collapsed on an overturned crate.

"You may stay as long as you like," Dragon Maker said, "but your father is not here."

Keung groaned with disappointment. How could he have been so stupid, thinking it would be easy, thinking his father would be here, waiting for him. "Do you know where he is?"

"They come and they go." Dragon Maker sighed. "I knew your father, Chan Sam. A good man. I wrote the letter for him and sent it to your mother. Sometime after that he had … difficulties, and left for the railway camps."

Keung's heart sank. "What difficulties?"

"Time enough for that," Dragon Maker replied. "You do not want to carry too many burdens so soon after your arrival."

"I'll leave tomorrow and begin my search along the railway."

Dragon Maker shook his head. "That would not be wise."

"What do you mean?" Keung asked.

"You have agreed to work for Blue-Scar Wong. And he is not a man you want to displease."

Chapter 7

It was raining the day of the Chinatown trip, a heavy rain that splashed the pavement with neon reflections and made the street shimmer. "I'll meet you at Fan Tan Alley at two o'clock," Val said as the school bus arrived. "Here's a note for your teacher." She gave Jasmine's braid a tug. "You look terrific," she said. "Have fun."

The class spilled off the bus and gathered in excited clusters in front of the restaurant. An assortment of red sweaters brightened the sidewalk, along with shirts decorated with dragons and Chinese writing.

"Hi Jasmine," said Krista, giving her a friendly wave. "Where did you get the clothes?"

"From my aunt. It's what the Chinese wore when they came to build the railway."

"I didn't know that," said Becky. "You look great. But don't you feel like, *weird*?"

"No," Jasmine replied. The question surprised her. "I feel right at home."

"Figures," Becky said. "You always have to be different. But you can sit with us anyway, okay?"

"Sure." Becky's words stung. Was there an edge to them she hadn't noticed before? Was she hearing things differently, or was she overly sensitive?

They're still my friends, she thought as they trooped up the stairs. *Even though I've gone quiet on them.* But something was missing — the easy warmth, the feeling of being accepted. She paused by the aquarium at the top of the stairs. Was she really so different? And if she was, so what? It didn't matter.

"Fish for abundance and prosperity," Becky said. "Right, Jasmine?"

"I think so." There were many symbols: a chicken for happiness, a cricket for good luck, a tortoise for long life. It was because of the language, Mrs. Butler had explained. If a word had the same sound as another word, then it took on the same meaning. Like the word for pear. Don't share a pear with a friend, because pear has the same sound as the word for departure. Had she shared a pear with her dad? No. Neither of them liked pears anyway.

Red was supposed to bring good luck. She had tied a red ribbon around her braid, hoping her dad's flight would be cancelled. Or maybe he'd have an accident. A little one, but serious enough for him to be sent home.

No sooner had they sat at the round table than the waiters began bringing food. Deep fried egg rolls, steamed dumplings stuffed with pork. Chop suey with water chestnuts, bamboo shoots, and beef. Bite-sized portions of pork in sweet-and-sour sauce. A plate of chow mein with diced chicken, fried noodles, and vegetables.

"This is hard to eat," Jasmine said as the beansprouts slipped from her chopsticks.

"You can come here with your aunt," said Krista. "You'll get lots of practice."

"Oh, I almost forgot." Jasmine took out the note and handed it to her teacher. "My aunt's meeting me at two o'clock in Fan Tan Alley, wherever that is."

"It's one of the stops on your scavenger hunt," said Mrs. Butler. "You'll find it easily enough."

At the end of the meal, the fortune cookies arrived. Becky read, "*You will travel a great distance.* You should've got this one, Jasmine, since your aunt's driving you to Sooke every day. What does yours say?"

"*Someone from your past will soon re-enter your life.*" *Good*, she thought. *Maybe Dad won't stay in China after all.*

Mrs. Butler was handing out the scavenger hunt lists. "Mark off the items as you find them. I'll meet everyone in front of the restaurant at two o'clock."

By the time they left the restaurant the rain had turned into a thick fog, enveloping them in the exotic atmosphere of Chinatown. On both sides of the street, shops displayed huge earthenware jars and vases painted with phoenixes or dragons. Outdoor stands offered a variety of fruits and vegetables, from lemon grass and winter melon to long stalks of sugar cane. Red posts topped with pagoda-shaped lanterns lined the street. Even the telephone booth had a pagoda roof. At the end of the block was the gate Jasmine had seen the night before, a brilliantly painted structure flanked by two stone lions. She checked it on her list: *Gate of Harmonious Interest.*

Every doorway opened into a different world. "Look at this," Krista said. She held up a bulky packet of paper money, used for burning on ancestors' graves. "When it burns, the smoke rises to heaven. Then the ancestors have money to spend."

They checked off pickled jellyfish, bins of white rice and black rice, fluttery black mushrooms, fish dried and flattened as thin as parchment.

In the herb shop they gasped at the overpowering smell of dried fish and lizards, animal parts, and strange plants used to treat ailments and allergies. "How do people eat them?" Jasmine wondered.

"Put them in stew or soup, or boil them in water and drink it like tea," the herbalist said. He held up a dried seahorse. "You want to try?"

"No thanks," they said.

In another store they found ink sticks and chopsticks, a poster showing the Great Wall covered with snow, and jade figures in all shades of green. But no white jade, Jasmine noticed. And no jade tigers.

"Here it is," Becky said suddenly, pointing to a signpost. "Fan Tan Alley. Isn't this where you're supposed to meet your aunt?"

"Yes, but I've still got fifteen minutes. I haven't even bought anything yet."

"Come on, you guys," Krista said excitedly. "This store is really cool."

The entrance was jammed with paper chains and streamers that cascaded from the ceiling like papery pagodas, brightly coloured in red, turquoise, green and gold. Jars and boxes crowded the shelves, stuffed with little toys and gadgets, from panda pencil sharpeners and tin whistles to Chinese dolls.

Krista led the way down a narrow passageway crowded with blue-and-white porcelain, Chinese junks, and statues of Buddha. It opened into another room, a jumble of cotton slippers, wicker baskets, straw hats, and slippery silk robes. "Hurry up," she called. "There's *another* room in this never-ending store."

They followed her along a dark and twisting passage into a larger room. "It's a kind of museum," she said. "See that guy in there? Doesn't he look real?" A mannequin dressed in a long black gown stood behind a wicket, counting out money. "This used to be a gambling den." She moved to a display case. "Where's the scavenger list? Check off tiles for playing mah jong, then we'll go down the alley."

"Hey, look!" Jasmine pointed to a pile of buttons and a brass cup. "It's a fan tan game," she said, reading the label. "That's how the alley got its name. See, the banker divides a pile of buttons into fours, and the players bet on how many will be left over."

"Too much like math," said Becky. "Now let's go. There's only one store left."

"Wait a minute," Jasmine said. A row of dragons leaping along a dusty shelf caught her eye. "I want to look at these."

"Catch up to us then." Krista and Becky headed back to the main entrance, while Jasmine turned her attention to the dragons. As she was reaching for the blue one, her eyes flicked over to the mannequin. It seemed as though he was watching her.

"You like the dragon?" A man appeared through a curtained doorway. "Brings good luck, the dragon. *Lung*, we call him. Come, I'll take your money. For you, that dragon is ten dollars. Very special."

Jasmine thought for a moment. Ten dollars was more than she wanted to spend, but … "Okay," she said impulsively, and handed him a $10 bill. "No tax?"

He laughed. "Not today!" he said. He wrapped the dragon carefully and placed it in a bag. "You want more luck?" He picked up a red envelope lying on the counter and placed a coin inside. "Here," he said. "*Lai see*, just for you."

"Thanks." Jasmine smiled. "This is lucky money, right?" She traced her fingers around the Chinese characters printed in gold on the envelope. "*Gung hey fat choy*!" she said.

"Yes! Happy New Year!" He studied her closely, smiling and nodding his head as if pleased with what he saw. "Happy New Year, Dragon Girl!"

How does he know I'm a Dragon Girl? And why does he keep staring at me? Must be the clothes, she decided. *That's all.*

As she was turning to go she noticed a small room that opened onto an alley. "Isn't that Fan Tan Alley?" She pointed to the *No Exit* sign hanging from the door. "Can I go out that way?"

"Yes, Fan Tan Alley!" He rubbed his hands together. "For you, the door will open. Exit, for good luck dragon." He took a key from his pocket and unlocked the door. "Goodbye, Dragon Girl."

Then he bowed to Jasmine as she walked through the door and into the alley.

Chapter 8

Something had changed. Jasmine knew it the instant the door closed behind her. The sounds were different. No traffic. No brakes, no horns, no whish of tires. And no people. No footsteps, no voices. A silence so heavy she could almost touch it.

She looked at her watch. Almost two o'clock, time to go. But which way? Mist curled around her, shutting out her surroundings. She had no sense of space, no sense of direction. What's more, the doorway she had passed through had disappeared. There was no way back.

With fumbling fingers she opened the *lai see* envelope. What had the man put inside? A silver coin, the size of a quarter. On one side was the portrait of a queen with the words VICTORIA DEI GRATIA REGINA CANADA. *Okay,* she thought. *Victoria is in Canada.* She turned the coin over. There were maple boughs etched along the edges, tied at the bottom with a ribbon and separated at the top by a crown. Beneath the crown were three lines: 25 CENTS 1881.

Eighteen eighty-one? Then Victoria must refer to the queen, not the place at all. But what did it mean? What had happened?

She sank to the ground and hugged herself tightly, thinking, *Don't panic, concentrate on your breathing. Tai chi breathing, from deep down….*

It was the smell that roused her, the stink of rotting garbage and raw sewage. And something else, a sweet, cloying smell, like boiled potatoes. She found herself in an alley, hemmed in by buildings on either side. She was sitting on the ground, leaning against a wall, surrounded by wooden boxes, crates, and piles of refuse. Overhead she could see a patch of sky, bright with stars. *I must have slept,* she thought, looking at her watch. It still said five minutes to two.

She was about to stand up when she heard footsteps. She crouched down, making herself as small as possible. Groups of men passed by. Some disappeared along narrow passages leading off the alley, others ducked through doorways. A thought struck her. *When you are a stranger, be invisible.* She took the red ribbon out of her hair and pulled down the brim of her hat. Then she slipped her watch inside her backpack and stashed it behind a pile of crates.

Think, she told herself. *If this really is 1881 then the door won't be there. But it could be the same building. All you have to do is find the right doorway....*

A crash broke into her thoughts. Angry voices rocked the alley. She froze as three men tore out of a doorway just ahead of her. With pigtails flying, they rushed past and vanished in the shadows.

"Worthless sons of dogs!" a man shouted after them. "Don't come back until you've found it!"

What are they looking for? Jasmine wondered, then stopped short. She could have sworn the man had spoken a Chinese dialect, but she had understood the words. How could that be? She didn't know any Chinese, apart from the New Year's greeting. She must have imagined it.

But she hadn't imagined the doorway. Cautiously, she peered inside. The dimly lit room smelled of smoke, sweat, liquor, and kerosene. Men of all ages crowded together, talking, laughing, throwing dice, and clacking dominoes. Fan tan players noisily placed their bets as dealers swept up piles of buttons. mah jong tiles clattered with the chatter of voices.

Through the smoky haze Jasmine saw several men clustered around a wicket. As one man stepped back, she caught a glimpse of the cashier. Her eyes widened. Surely that wasn't — No. That other cashier was a dummy. This one was real. But the room in the never-ending store had been a gambling den. This must be the same place. And somewhere, there was a way back.

Unnoticed, she crept past a boy sweeping up bits of debris and broken glass. No, not glass. China. One green piece looked like the curling tail of a dragon.

"Come on, Useless. Sweep it all up."

This time there was no mistake. It was the voice she'd heard in the alley, speaking the same Chinese dialect. And she could understand the words.

The scar-faced man shook his fist at the boy and scowled. Like the others, he wore his hair in one long pigtail. But instead of the dark pants and quilted jacket worn by the others, this man wore an embroidered robe, along with an air of arrogance and authority. He consulted with the cashier from time to time and strutted from table to table overseeing the various games. Jasmine noticed how the players cowered under his scrutiny, and breathed more easily when he moved on.

Suddenly, he grabbed a player by his jacket and lifted him out of his chair. "Take this message to your worthless son," he snarled. "No one tries to trick Blue-Scar Wong. He has three days to pay his debt. Hear that, old man? Three days."

"Leave him alone!" The boy gripped the broom and boldly faced the older man.

Blue-Scar spun around, his face contorted with anger.

"Do not interfere with me," he said, his voice hard as steel. He drew a knife from the folds of his sleeve and waved it at the boy. "Your time is running out, too."

Unflinching, the boy stared back. In his eyes, Jasmine recognized something familiar. Or was it someone? She remembered the boy in her dream, standing alone on the crowded ship. Remembered, too, how his eyes had seemed to pull her in. Was this the boy? And if so, was she meant to be here? She slid to the floor, frightened without knowing why.

"Bah!" Blue-Scar spat with contempt. "Get back to your work."

As he stormed away, Jasmine looked up and found the boy gazing at her with an incredulous look on his face, a look that clearly said: *I know you.* Then he shook his head as if clearing it of dreams and went back to his sweeping.

The swell of voices rose steadily as the night wore on. Shouts of joy mingled with cries of despair as winners and losers continued to play.

But the presence of Blue-Scar Wong clouded the room. Once, Jasmine felt his eyes burning into her. She buried her face in her arms, terrified that he would expose her as the stranger she was. *Maybe he'll think I'm asleep and leave me alone. Or he'll throw me out. Or make me get up and gamble.* But before he could confront her, a fight broke out, demanding his attention. She breathed a sigh of relief and shifted to a pile of crates. Half hidden, she trembled alone in the dingy room, trying to think of a way out.

When she opened her eyes, the room was quiet and cold. Lamps had been extinguished, leaving behind a thick pall of smoke. Light filtered through the open doorway. Only the boy remained.

He stood in the doorway staring at her, rubbing his eyes in disbelief. Wasn't this the face he'd seen in his dreams? And if so, it was a *girl* crouching there on the floor, not another coolie. But how could that be? The face in his dreams belonged to Bright Jade, a spirit from another time. This girl was real. And she was *here,* in *his* time. *I'll put her to the test,* he decided. Turning abruptly, he bolted into the alley.

Jasmine leaped up and followed. Down the alley, through passageways and courtyards, twisting through a maze enclosed by huts, crudely built sheds, and tumbledown fences. Weathered shacks tottered on pilings or on top of each other, leaning crazily this way and that in a desperate attempt to stay upright. They reminded her of tattered people, supporting each other as they peered warily at the world through tiny, grime-streaked windows.

She kept the boy in sight as he dashed between pilings, over rickety bridges held up by stilts, over muddy ground soaked with rain and waste water, over narrow passages clogged with garbage.

How will I find my way out of here? she wondered, wishing she'd left a trail of crumbs like Hansel and Gretel. *And where is he going, to the witch? Or worse?* She felt a prickle of fear, but there was no question of turning back. Something was pulling her, some force she couldn't explain.

The boy darted into another courtyard, with a chicken coop and a patch of dirt for growing vegetables. A rooster crowed and hens began clucking. Somewhere a dog barked. Someone shouted. Jasmine ducked under several lines of laundry and followed the boy up a staircase that snaked its way along the back of a wooden building. Up one flight, then another and another, until he stopped in front of a red door, panting and out of breath.

"Whew!" Jasmine gasped. She brushed past him and leaned against the door. Two faded posters partially hid the peeling red paint. "Door Guardians," she said, recognizing the fierce warriors she'd seen in a book. "To keep away evil spirits and unwanted guests."

Then she smiled, her eyes bright with wonder. For the words sliding over her tongue were Cantonese, and she was speaking it as if she'd spoken it all her life.

The boy gaped, his thoughts in a turmoil. The girl had passed the test, had followed him around all sorts of sharp angles and curves when everyone knows spirits can only travel in straight lines. So, she wasn't a spirit. But if she wasn't Bright Jade, who was she? How was it she could speak his dialect? And where had she come from? Perhaps Dragon Maker would know. He opened the door and stepped in.

Jasmine followed, her nerves tingling with excitement. The room smelled of incense. A pot-bellied stove stood in one corner, its crooked chimney climbing through a hole in the ceiling. Dragons danced along the shelves and tumbled across the battered table. A man stood with his back to her, bent over —

Déjà vu. Her aunt's words came back. She knew the man was old, knew his skin was burnished the colour of copper. She knew he held three lighted sticks of incense, knew he would place them in a cup of earth before a small altar.

And so he did. Then he turned and said, "Welcome, Jasmine. Welcome, Dragon Girl. I am the one they call Dragon Maker, as you can see." His weather-beaten face cracked in a smile.

Jasmine drew back, puzzled. "How did you know my name?"

His eyes pierced her, as if looking for something. "I have known you in another time," he said. "And you have been expected."

"Expected for what?"

"You will know in time." He turned to the boy. "Keung, give her some soup. She needs to eat something and rest awhile."

Jasmine breathed in the aroma of herbs, surprised at how hungry she felt. When she finished the soup, Dragon Maker handed her a cup of fragrant tea. Delicate white petals floated on top. She took a sip, remembering the first time she had tasted it, the night before her father went away. "I bought some jasmine tea for you," he'd said, "so when you drink it you'll think of me in China." She refused to speak or even look at him. As soon as he left the room, she'd poured it down the sink.

A wave of exhaustion washed over her. Had the boy put a sleeping potion in her soup? Some herbs caused drowsiness. Maybe powdered crickets were in the soup, or worse. Maybe Dragon Maker's voice had hypnotized her, put her in a trance. Her head drooped. Her eyelids felt heavy.

The boy took her arm and led her into a room no bigger than a closet. A mat lay on the plank floor. She curled up on it as the boy covered her with a quilt. "Who are you?" she asked sleepily. "Why are you here?"

"I'm Chan Tai Keung. I've come to find my father."

"I've lost my father, too," she said. "And my mother." Her face crumpled and she felt the sting of tears. She closed her eyes and drifted off to sleep.

Bright Jade was waiting in the garden. "It has been a long journey," she said. "But remember, a journey of a thousand miles begins with a single step."

"And a journey of a thousand years begins with a single dream," said Jasmine.

"This was my tiger," Bright Jade said, holding out the amulet. "But I have lost him and cannot rest until he is found." Tears streamed down her face as the white jade turned to dust in her hand. "There have been many deaths and there will be many more. Such is the curse of the white jade tiger. I am sorry." Slowly she turned and walked away.

"Wait," called Jasmine. "What does this have to do with me?"

Bright Jade did not answer. Jasmine followed her out of the room, down the staircase, through the maze of shacks, and into the alley. There, the spirit vanished.

Chapter 9

"Here she is! Jasmine, what happened?" Voices floated through the fog. Voices coming closer, calling her back.

She looked up to find a group of classmates standing over her, their faces creased with worry. "What happened?" asked Becky. "Did you fall or something?"

"Get up, Jasmine," said Krista. "It's two o'clock, time to go."

"Two? It can't be. There wasn't time for all that to happen. I couldn't have spent the night —" Their bewildered looks made her stop.

"What are you talking about? What night? For all what to happen?"

"Nothing." She tried to stand, steadying herself against the brick wall, but fell back, overcome by dizziness.

"Are you okay?" Becky leaned over and helped her up. "You look like you're going to pass out."

"My head feels funny, that's all." She blinked a few times, trying to focus on her surroundings. She was definitely in Fan Tan Alley. There was the doorway. And there was a passage leading off the alley. Was that where she had gone? "My backpack," she remembered suddenly. "I left it behind some crates."

"Relax, it's right here." Krista handed it to her. "You must have dropped it when you fell. Now come on. Your aunt's waiting."

Jasmine took one last look around, hoping to see — what? She wasn't sure. But before leaving the alley she thought she heard a voice calling her name. She glanced over her shoulder in time to see a dark figure staring in her direction. Although it was partially hidden by mist, she couldn't help but notice the outstretched arm entreating her to stay.

Keung was frantic. He had seen the girl steal out of the room and down the stairs. Desperately he followed as she skimmed through the labyrinth of shacks and passages, back to the alley. "Jasmine, come back!" he cried, holding out his hand. But before he could say another word, she had vanished.

"Where did she come from?" he asked. "And how could she vanish like that if she wasn't a spirit? Was it all a dream? Did you put opium in my tea?"

"No, no," Dragon Maker assured him. "You have not been dreaming."

"Why does she look so foreign? She wears the same clothes I do, yet she is like —"

"A barbarian!" Dragon Maker chuckled. "Like the dragon, Bright Jade's spirit can take many forms. Who can foretell the kaleidoscope of changes over two thousand years? A spirit changes and seeks many different homes. Do not worry. All is as it should be." He continued shaping a new dragon that leaped in the clouds.

"Will she come back?"

"Of course. But only when you least expect it. So get back to the restaurant before Blue-Scar takes a stick to you. Go on, now. Go!" Gently, he shoved the boy from the room and returned to his clay.

"How was Chinatown?" Val asked as they were driving home.

"Well … different from what I'd expected."

"It is different."

"Do you spend much time there?"

"Oh, yes, I've always loved Chinatown. That's one of the reasons I bought this condo. It's so close. How did your clothes work out, by the way?"

"Great. I blended right in."

"There were others wearing the same thing?"

"Lots," she said, smiling. "And they all had one long braid." Well, it was true. She had blended in. She could have been invisible, for all the attention they'd paid her. Except for Keung. And that horrible man with the scar. "Have you ever …" She was tempted to tell her aunt, but something made her pause.

"What?"

"Oh, nothing." She wouldn't say anything yet. Not until things were clearer in her own mind. Better let Val get used to her, before thinking she had a crazy kid on her hands.

Back in her room, she took off the coolie clothes and placed them on the window seat. It *was* Keung she'd seen in her dream, she was sure of it. Why hadn't she talked to him? All that time wasted. She'd have to go back. But how?

She took out the quarter. Maybe the coin triggered her passage into 1881. Or was it the man with the key? Or the dragon? She dusted it off with the corner of her shirt and set it on the dresser. Tomorrow she'd go to Chinatown and try again. Meanwhile, she'd browse through her aunt's books, then work on the quilt. And try to figure out the new puzzle in her life.

The room had a pine bookcase along one wall, stuffed with hundreds of books, carefully organized by subjects. *Trust Val,* Jasmine thought, chuckling. She could hear her father saying, "She'll probably make you sign them out, issue you a card." Well, she'd been a librarian, after all. Mythology, superstitions, Canadian history, shelf after shelf of adventure and travel, and books on China: history, art, folktales, dragons. She pulled one off the shelf, sat on the window seat, and began turning pages.

In no time she was lost in dragon lore. There were five types: a heavenly dragon that guarded the mansions of the gods, a spiritual dragon that controlled winds and rains, an earthly dragon that cleared rivers and deepened seas, an imperial dragon with five claws, and dragons that guarded hidden treasure. Which one are you? she asked her blue-glazed dragon. She stared at it, willing it to respond in some way. Just when she was sure it was going to, Val called out from the kitchen, "Dinner's ready."

Jasmine looked at her watch in disbelief. Six o'clock already? There was no way to figure out the passing of time.

Val's eyes lit up when she saw the dragon. "Where did you get this?" she asked, running her fingers over the rippling tail.

"In that never-ending store in Chinatown. It was in the museum room, the one that used to be a gambling den."

"Were there any others?"

"A whole shelf, up above the display case. They were really dusty, like they'd been there a long time."

Val sat on the edge of the bed, examining the dragon closely. "I'll bet you ten to one this was made by the Dragon Maker."

Jasmine tried to hide her excitement. "Dragon Maker?"

Val nodded. "He lived in Chinatown in the early 1900s. Made dragons out of clay and sold them. Apparently, he used to hide things inside his dragons, so if one got broken, the owner would find something else. To make up for the loss, I suppose."

Jasmine remembered the broken china in the gambling den, the piece that resembled a dragon's tail. That must have been why it was smashed. Someone was looking for something. "What did he put inside?"

"Nothing of value. A tiny clay fisherman or a piece of silk. Once someone found a cotton slipper wedged inside. Maybe your dragon has the other one."

"Wouldn't the stuff burn up when the clay was fired?"

"No, because after he shaped the dragon he cut it in half, hollowed it out and fired the halves separately. Then he put the secret inside and joined the pieces together." She pointed to a faint line. "See? There's the join."

Jasmine shook the dragon. "Wouldn't you be able to hear something rattling?"

"Not with our Dragon Maker. He didn't want to give away any secrets, so he'd wrap things up in scraps of cloth."

"How do you know all this?"

"It's a story that I heard in Chinatown years ago. All the old-timers knew it. Not anymore though, not since the dragons disappeared. Funny you should have seen them. Someone must have unearthed them from somewhere, I suppose."

"Did you ever see one before?"

"Nope. Yours is the first. I spent a lot of time in Chinatown when I was a kid. My parents didn't like it but I went anyway. I even learned to speak a bit of Cantonese. My dad almost hit the roof when he found out."

Jasmine looked at her aunt in surprise. A rebel! "Why didn't your parents like you going there?"

"It was different in those days. Forbidding and mysterious. Alleys and passageways, strange sights and sounds and smells. I loved it. I always felt I was looking for something in Chinatown, but I never knew what it was. So I never found it."

"Maybe it was the dragon," Jasmine said. "We could go tomorrow." A thought struck her. "It's already tomorrow in China, isn't it? Will Dad be okay, do you think?" *Even though I still hate him,* she added silently.

"Of course. And I'm sure he'll call soon."

"Maybe I'll send him a postcard from Chinatown, once I know where he's staying." In spite of her anger, it was a horrible feeling, not knowing. She thought of Keung, alone in a strange land, looking for his father. He must have felt empty, too. As if a part of himself had been cut away.

Val set a brisk pace across the Johnson Street Bridge. Jasmine was glad she had long legs, otherwise she'd never be able to keep up. Her aunt was turning out to be a human dynamo as well as a former rebel.

"Isn't it nice to see the sun for a change?" Val said brightly.

Jasmine agreed, but secretly wished it was misty. Maybe the mist had something to do with her experience the day before.

Traffic hummed over the steel deck of the bridge. "There's a warning before the bridge goes up, isn't there?" she asked, glancing nervously at the operator's shed.

"Not on Saturdays," Val teased.

They strode along Store Street, past restaurants, galleries, and warehouses, before turning up Fisgard. "Here it is, the never-ending store."

"Perfect name," Val said. She led the way through the small rooms and connecting hallways, exclaiming over items she remembered from past visits and offering a running commentary on anything that took her fancy. Jasmine only half listened, eager to get to the dragons. Finally they reached the back room.

"Now then. Somewhere in here?" Val asked.

"Uh-huh, right above —" She stopped, stunned to see a bare brick wall. "The shelf was right there. With a whole row of dragons on it."

"Are you sure? Maybe they were in another part of the room."

"No!" Her voice sounded too loud, too frantic. "I know they were there." She approached the clerk behind the counter. "Do you know what happened to the dragons? They were on a shelf above the display case."

The clerk shook her head. "There's never been a shelf there that I can remember. We've got lots of dragons at the front of the store."

"But they were in this room," Jasmine insisted. "The man who was here yesterday, is he around?"

"Who? A man that was shopping?"

"No, he was working here. He sold me the dragon and gave me a *lai see* envelope with a coin in it."

The clerk sighed, exasperated. "I was here myself yesterday, all day, except for my lunch break. It was a busy day. Lots of school kids." She flashed a look at Val, and turned to Jasmine. "Maybe you dreamed it."

Jasmine twisted her braid, trying to hide her confusion. "What time was your lunch break?"

"I left about 1:30."

So, Jasmine thought. *You weren't even here when I bought the dragon. That man could have been here without your knowing. He'd come from behind....* She stared blankly at the wall in the far corner of the room. The curtained doorway wasn't there either.

But the doorway opening onto Fan Tan Alley was there, and so was the *No Exit* sign. "Can we go out that way?"

"Sure," said the clerk. "Don't know why we keep leaving that sign up."

Jasmine took a deep breath and opened the door, hoping to find Keung waiting on the other side. But she didn't. Whatever magic had been at work the day before was gone.

"Where to now?" Val asked. "It's a bit early for lunch, but why not?"

"Sure." Jasmine smiled, grateful her aunt wasn't pestering her with questions or treating her like some crazy person. She knew the dragon was real. It had come from somewhere.

She'd try again, and do it right. Like a detective, she'd set things up exactly the way they'd been the first time, right down to the red ribbon in her hair. Humming to herself, she plunged into the chicken chow mein while fine-tuning her plan. Even the chopsticks co-operated.

Chapter 10

The Year of the Snake gusted into the Year of the Horse — 1882. That New Year's Day was a windy one in Victoria, so windy the Chinese were warned not to explode the traditional fireworks. Still, Keung and Dragon Maker burned incense and placed a sweet offering in front of the Kitchen God, hoping he would carry a good report to the Jade Emperor. Then they removed his soot-smeared image from behind the stove and replaced it with a bright new one. "Now the scrolls," Dragon Maker said as he handed Keung the long strips of red paper.

Keung was surprised. "Do you think I'm ready?"

Dragon Maker set the ink stone and brushes before the boy. "You are an excellent pupil," he said proudly, "with a great capacity for learning. Soon we will begin English lessons. But for now, let me see the characters for prosperity, longevity and good fortune."

"*Gung hey fat choy*!" Keung beamed with pleasure and began to write, making sure each brush stroke was perfect. His mother would be so proud. If only she could see these New Year scrolls hanging on the door. And his father …

Keung could feel his concentration slipping. As his brush glided over the paper, he tried to unravel the worries from his mind. But the more he unravelled, the more tangled up they became.

First there was the girl, the spirit who was not a spirit. Throughout the long autumn he had visited the spot where he had last seen her, hoping she would reappear. But she had not. "Why hasn't she come back?" he asked.

"She will come when the time is right," said Dragon Maker, "not before. Bright Jade has been with us two thousand years, long enough to learn patience. But her spirit is restless, and I do not think it will be long."

Then there was his father. Railway construction eased off during the winter months and the population of Chinatown had grown. In January men thronged into Victoria, waiting to return to China to spend Chinese New Year with their families. Each night they packed themselves into the cramped shacks. And each night, Keung asked the same questions. "Do you know my father, Chan Sam? He came in the Year of the Tiger and went to work on the railway. Have you seen him?"

Being sons and fathers themselves, cut off from their homes and families, they sympathized with Keung but could not help him. "There are many camps along the river," they said. "Your father could be in any one of them. He could be working in Yale or mining for gold in a worked-out claim. Go to the Fraser Canyon and ask there."

They also spoke of the men who would never return. "Perhaps your father is one of those," they said. "Perhaps he is one of the nameless corpses left in the canyon without proper burial."

Keung shook his head. "I would know if he was dead. His spirit would tell me."

"Very well then," they said. "Let his spirit guide you to him. We have sorrows of our own."

Then there was the problem of Blue-Scar Wong. For Keung, it seemed, was not the only one searching for Chan Sam. "Why is Blue-Scar so interested in my father?" he wondered aloud. "Each day he asks about him. Where is he? When is he coming back? But when I say I must go and look for him, Blue-Scar won't let me. 'You must first earn back the money I sent to your mother,' he says. So all day I work in his restaurant and all night in his gambling den!" He threw the brush down angrily. "I feel like a tiger in a cage."

Dragon Maker calmly shaped the head of his dragon. "I have not told you because I promised your father. But perhaps it was not a wise promise." He turned to face the boy. "Blue-Scar wants what he must not have. The white jade tiger."

Keung's heart beat fast and hard. The tiger! So absorbed had he been with his other problems, he had completely forgotten the amulet. "You know about the tiger?"

Dragon Maker nodded. "Your father arrived in Victoria during the Year of the Tiger. At that time, the Chinese had to buy a licence to stay. Every three months the tax collector would storm into Chinatown with a bailiff and seize the belongings of anyone who did not have a licence. Ordinary people as well as merchants had their goods loaded up and taken to the police barracks. Chests of tea, bales of cloth, packages of opium and boxes of personal effects were piled up for public sale. Many dragons ended up in that pile," he said. "And from your father they took a white jade tiger."

"But how did —"

"Wait," Dragon Maker said, raising his hand. "We did not accept this tax. Instead of paying it, we organized a strike. Not a single Chinese went to work. Not a cannery worker, factory worker, laundry worker, or shoemaker. Not one! Wealthy white ladies had to do their own housework, hotel owners did their own cooking and cursed the shortage of clean napkins. Men sawed their own wood and polished their own boots. It was a great inconvenience for them." He chuckled.

"The strike lasted five days. Then the government learned it could not keep the tax anyway, and the goods had to be returned. But the bailiff had already sold many belongings. And who do you suppose bought the jade tiger?"

"Blue-Scar Wong!" Keung exclaimed. "But how did my father get it back?"

"Your father sometimes worked in Blue-Scar's opium den. One night, while Blue-Scar was drifting away on an opium dream, Chan Sam saw his chance. He caught a glimpse of the tiger in the folds of Blue-Scar's robe and he took it. Right away he came to me, afraid that once Blue-Scar found out, his life would be in danger. I advised him to go to the Fraser Canyon and lose himself amongst the railway workers. I offered to hide the tiger for him, but he refused. This is the first place Wong will look, he said.

"He was right. The next morning Blue-Scar and his men tore my room apart, searching for the tiger. They smashed all my dragons, thinking I'd hidden it inside one of them. But they never found it. 'Go,' I told them. 'The dragon has devoured the tiger, but it is not one of these.'"

"Why does Blue-Scar want it so badly?"

"Because it is priceless. But it must be returned to Bright Jade," Dragon Maker said firmly. "Only the return of the tiger can end the curse."

Keung frowned. "I don't understand. How did my father get it in the first place?"

Dragon Maker looked away, as if reluctant to speak. Finally he said, "The tiger was swept from Bright Jade's grave during the floods. Many years later Chan Sam found it buried in the mud. He kept it as a talisman. When he left for Gold Mountain he took it with him."

"My father kept it?" Keung was stunned. What would he tell his mother? That his own father had found the tiger and unleashed the curse on his family? He could never tell her that. He was too ashamed.

After much thought, Keung wrote to his mother and told her that all was well. Dragon Maker was teaching him to read and write. He was earning a fortune in the restaurant, he would soon see his father, he would surely be home to welcome in the Year of the Sheep. Then he signed his name, hoping the gods would forgive him for not being entirely truthful.

Chapter 11

"Your dad's on the phone."

Jasmine buried her face in the covers, pretending to be asleep. So, he's made it to China. He'll give Val his address and he won't be lost in my mind anymore. But I won't talk to him. Then she thought of Keung. Did he ever find his father? Or was he lost forever? And here she was, sulking.

In an instant her mind was made up. "Coming!" She leaped out of bed and rushed to the phone. "Hi, Dad." She tried to sound cool and indifferent, but he *was* calling from across the world.

He told her a letter was on the way so he'd keep the conversation short. Was everything fine? Yes, yes. "I miss you, Dad." Then, so she wouldn't sound too soppy, "But only because you make great lasagna."

"Wait'll you try my sauteed eel and steamed sea cucumbers."

"Dad! Yuck!"

"How was your Chinatown trip? Did it make you want to join me?"

"It was … yeah, I might want to come. It sort of depends. I'll see, okay?"

"Okay, honey, whatever you decide is fine with me. I love you. Write soon. Bye."

"Bye, Dad." Breaking the connection was hard. There was so much she wanted to say. But how could she tell him she was planning to go back to Chinatown and didn't know how long she'd be gone? How could she tell him about the doorway in the never-ending store, or the gambling den in Fan Tan Alley, or Keung and Dragon Maker? It wasn't the sort of thing you casually mention on the phone, especially not on a long-distance call.

The figure floated above the river. "Wait," Jasmine cried, struggling to keep up. But the figure floated on upstream, heedless of the swirling eddies and whirlpools of muddy water.

As Jasmine stumbled along the shoreline, ghostly images began to appear. They rose from the water and drifted down from the towering cliffs. Hundreds of ghosts, strangely calm in the crash and whirl of the river.

Soon the figure reached a passage in the steep-walled canyon. It raised a hand, halting the surge of ghosts. Then slowly it turned.

"Bright Jade!" Jasmine exclaimed. "You've come back."

"No, Jasmine. It's you that's come back." Bright Jade hovered above the river, her arms outstretched as if to embrace the ghosts who followed. She looked frail, poised above the rapids. But at the same time, it seemed as though she could stop the river with a stroke of her hand.

"Where are you going?" Jasmine asked.

"We are going through Hell's Gate." She spoke in a whisper, yet her words resounded off the canyon walls.

"Wait for me!" Jasmine tried to follow, but the ghosts blocked her passage. A roar stormed down from the granite walls and thundered through the canyon. Before her eyes the ghosts swirled into one image, a leaping tiger that roared with such sorrow and fury Jasmine covered her ears and screamed.

Suddenly the room was flooded with light. Her aunt leaned over her bed. "Jasmine! What's wrong?"

"A dream … the tiger …" Her voice trembled. "Have you ever heard of Hell's Gate?"

If Val was surprised by the question she didn't show it. "Well, it could mean the gate outside of Hell, I suppose, if there is such a thing. Or it could be in the Fraser Canyon, where the river goes through a narrow passage. Is that what your dream was about?"

"Sort of." She took a deep breath. "Did a lot of Chinese people live in the Fraser Canyon?"

"Heavens, yes. Thousands of Chinese lived there when they were building the Canadian Pacific Railway."

"And a lot of them died?"

"Hundreds." Val patted Jasmine lightly on the brow. "Think you can go back to sleep now?"

"Uh-huh," Jasmine murmured, snuggling beneath the covers. "Now I know where I have to go."

Next morning Jasmine tucked the *lai see* envelope and dragon into her backpack. She put on a dark shirt, the coolie pants, and the jacket. Then she braided her hair and placed the hat on her head. Everything was exactly the same, right down to the cotton shoes and red ribbon.

"You're going to Chinatown," Val said.

"It's okay, isn't it? I know how to get there and I won't stay long."

"Sure. Just promise you'll stay out of trouble."

"Hey, Trouble's my middle name. At least that's what Dad says. I'll send him a postcard of Chinatown, now that I've got his address. Do you want anything?"

"Could you get some gunpowder tea? It comes in a little green box." She handed Jasmine a $20 bill. "The grocery store near the corner has it."

"Okay. I might get some fortune cookies, too."

"You seem chipper this morning, in spite of the nightmare."

"Oh, that was no nightmare. That was a message."

She reached the never-ending store at ten o'clock.

"Good morning," the clerk said, smiling at her appearance.

"Hi!" Jasmine smiled in return and made her way to the back room. There was the mannequin, there was the display case, and there was the brick wall. No shelf, no dragons, no curtained doorway.

Never mind, she told herself, trying not to feel discouraged. *It's not over yet.* She headed for the doorway with the *No Exit* sign. "Can I get out this way?" she asked.

The young man reading behind the counter didn't even look up. "Go ahead," he said.

Heart pounding, she opened the door.

And there he was, standing in the grey dawn of the alley. "Jasmine! At last you've come!"

Her heart skipped with joy. He was waiting for her. He had known she would come.

"I've waited so long," he said.

Jasmine laughed. "It's only been two days. I tried yesterday, but couldn't get through."

"Yesterday?" He frowned. "But … I've waited many months. Almost a year without a sign, not even in a dream."

Jasmine was puzzled. "What year is this?"

"The Year of the Horse," he said. "When you first came it was October 1881. Now it's the end of August 1882."

So, there was no connection between her time and his time, not in days or months or years. Come to think of it, he did look a bit older. Taller and leaner. And there were faint creases on his brow. From worry? From sadness? "Are you all right?" she asked.

"Yes," he said hesitantly. The muscles in his face tightened. "No. I haven't found my father. I haven't enough money to return home. And there is no Gold Mountain. It's all a lie."

"I'm sorry," Jasmine said. "I wish I —" With a flash of inspiration she removed the red ribbon and handed it to him. "Maybe this will bring good luck."

"Thank you," he said. His dimples flashed in a smile.

As he led her through Chinatown, he said, "It's strange that you appeared just now. I'm leaving today."

She nodded. "You're going to the Fraser Canyon, aren't you?" Then, as if it were the most natural thing in the world, she said, "I'm coming with you."

Keung burst into Dragon Maker's shack. "She's come back," he exclaimed. "But she wants to come with me!" He threw his hands in the air. "It's impossible!"

Dragon Maker beamed. "Jasmine! You have returned in time to leave again. But first, both of you, sit down and eat before your journey." He set before them bowls of rice and a platter of meat-filled dumplings, then poured steaming cups of tea. As they were eating he studied Jasmine closely, tilting his head from side to side.

His scrutiny was unsettling. Finally Jasmine flung down her chopsticks, unable to ignore it any longer. "I have to go! I can blend in, I know I can. No one in the gambling den noticed me. I'm dressed like all the other coolies." She pointed to Keung. "I look just like *him*!"

"Her eyes are foreign and she has a big nose," Keung retorted. "And she's a girl!"

"Her eyes do have a foreign look about them," Dragon Maker agreed, "but they are as dark as yours. Her skin is tanned and she is tall. Almost as tall as you, Keung. She wears the clothes of a coolie and her hands are not too soft." Jasmine rubbed her calluses and congratulated herself for learning to chop wood.

Dragon Maker pulled down the brim of her hat. "If you keep it low, the shadow will hide your eyes and hopefully your nose. There is nothing else we can do about the nose."

"It's not that big," Jasmine said. "Don't worry, I'll stay out of the way. And don't worry because I'm a girl. Times have changed, you know." She spoke so emphatically neither Keung nor Dragon Maker dared to ask what she meant.

"A fiery spirit!" Dragon Maker chuckled. "Tread cautiously with this one, Keung. And see that she doesn't talk too much." He picked up her backpack and frowned at the strange assortment of zippered pockets, buckles, and straps. "You cannot take this, not if you wish to be inconspicuous." He pointed to her watch. "Leave that behind. It would attract too much attention." He filled a cotton bag with a variety of useful items, attached it to a bamboo pole, and gave it to her. "Here is your bag and some money," he said, handing Keung a small pouch.

"We'll return," said Keung, "no matter what we find."

"Be careful," Dragon Maker said gravely. "Your eyes are not the only ones seeking the white jade tiger."

Jasmine was astonished by Dragon Maker's words. "The white jade tiger," she said as they set out. "I know about it from my dreams. But how does Dragon Maker know about it? And what does it have to do with you?"

"My father has the tiger. That's why it's so important to return it to Bright Jade's grave. To end this wretched curse on my family." He explained how his father had found it and kept it. And how Blue-Scar Wong wanted it.

"But Blue-Scar will know where you've gone. He'll follow you. Us, I mean. We'll lead him right to it."

"Not if we're careful. And he'll be looking for me alone. Maybe it is a good thing you're coming."

But Jasmine remembered the night in the gambling den, and felt certain Keung was wrong. Blue-Scar *would* be looking for both of them. In his eyes, she wasn't just another coolie.

Chapter 12

Chinatown was waking up. Voices rose from the ravine, from the dirt road, from storefronts, from the hidden recesses of shacks and alleys, from wooden balconies projecting over the boardwalks. Horses pulling watercarts stirred up clouds of dust, and peddlers hurried by with baskets slung on poles, filled with fish or vegetables. Men carrying loads of clean laundry strode out of Chinatown to make deliveries, their bamboo poles bending up and down across their shoulders.

Jasmine studied their faces. Some were dark tan, some were pale, even paler than hers. Some were full and round, some were thin and angular with high cheekbones. Everyone had dark eyes. Everyone had a pigtail. Many were short, so being tall for her age made her roughly the same size. And they all wore baggy pants and loose jackets like hers. She didn't feel the least bit conspicuous.

But one thing did strike her as odd. "There aren't any women. No girls, anywhere."

"Only merchants can afford to bring their wives from China," Keung said, "and they keep them inside their homes. Otherwise they might be kidnapped."

The air was filled with the smells of fish, drying seaweed, herbs, and vegetables frying in hot oil. Through it all drifted the sweetish odour Jasmine had noticed before. Boiling potatoes? Or was it more like roasted peanuts? "What is that smell?" she asked.

"Opium," Keung replied. "Raw opium is cooked here, in sheds behind the stores."

"Cooked?"

He nodded. "In boiling water for about twelve hours, until it turns to jelly. Then it's put in cans and sold."

"But opium's a drug. Isn't it against the law?"

Keung looked surprised. "No, it's a very important business. Very profitable. There are many opium factories here and many opium dens."

A frenzy of sawing and hammering caught Jasmine's attention, and she looked up the street to see a building under construction.

"That's the new Chinese theatre," Keung explained. "It might be finished when we come back. Then we'll see some Chinese opera."

They made their way along the waterfront, crowded with wharves and buildings. Importers and wholesale dealers sold provisions from Europe and the Far East, and proudly advertised their ability to fill orders for everything from codfish to candles to coal oil. Horses waited outside brick buildings or trotted along the road pulling wagons, carriages, and hacks of every description. Well-dressed gentlemen in bowler hats passed Aboriginals carrying bags of clams and sacks of salmon. A herd of cattle was being driven along Wharf Street, their bellows mingling with the shrieking blasts of boat whistles in the harbour.

Soon they reached the Hudson's Bay Company wharf where the *William Irving* was docked. Keung paid for their tickets — $1 each for deck passage to Yale.

As they boarded the sternwheeler, Jasmine could feel the stares of the white passengers. Two men blocked their way to the stern, one burly, the other one tall with a hawk-like face. "Make way for the Celestials," Burly snickered. But neither man moved, forcing them to duck under a lifeboat and clamber over coils of rope to get by.

"Finest steamer of the day, the *William Irving*," Jasmine heard Burly remark. "Built in 1880. A real beauty. First trip, you should've seen the fuss. Flags and twenty-one-gun salutes at every stop along the river. And Captain Irving passing out free beer and whisky like there was no tomorrow. Even had a band! Once the currents got rough the band eased off some, I can tell you."

Passengers continued to stream aboard the stern-wheeler, many heading for cabins and salons. Freight was loaded on too, including the herd of cattle.

Finally, the high-pitched screech of the steam whistle signaled the boat's departure. Across the harbour, Jasmine saw that the Johnson Street Bridge was gone. Only a footbridge connected the town to the First Nation settlement, where her aunt now lived. The Legislative Buildings were gone too, at least the ones she knew. In their place were the wood and brick structures she'd seen in pictures, the ones known as the "Birdcages."

And the Empress Hotel was gone! A wooden bridge crossed the bay and mudflats where the Empress and Causeway now stood. From the number of tin cans and bottles in the mud, it looked as though the place was used as a dumping ground. And that's where they built that ritzy hotel? She couldn't believe it.

The red brick Customs House was there, perched prominently on the waterfront. It looked large and grand, not dwarfed by high-rises and office blocks. And one distant landmark was familiar. "Look," she cried happily, pointing to the hills west of Victoria. "That's where I'm from. And they still look the same."

Keung looked at her strangely, but said nothing.

"Dangerous way to travel." The burly man's voice carried over the swish of water as the steamer headed into the strait. "Remember the *Fort Yale* back in sixty-one? Blown to shambles, she was."

"Boiler explosion, wasn't it? Two miles above Hope. Yessir, the captain and four passengers were beyond hope, that time."

Burly laughed. "Blown to shambles, along with the Indians and Chinamen. How many? Oh gosh, I dunno. Indians and Chinamen were never counted."

Jasmine felt a slow rage begin to simmer. How could they talk like that?

"Course, you have to expect explosions from time to time," Hawk-face said. "Boilers aren't made too sturdy. And captains like to go full-steam ahead with the safety valve held down tight." Burly stepped closer to Jasmine. Quickly, she lowered her head. "You're looking mighty nervous there, John. Afraid this steamer's gonna blow? We'll have chop suey then, all right."

She glanced at Keung but his face was unreadable.

Burly laughed and yanked on her braid. "Course, if you don't like it, you can go home."

Hawk-face joined in the laughter. "Wish they'd all go home."

Jasmine's face burned, in spite of the cool breeze blowing off the water. She dug her nails into her clenched fists, afraid the rage would boil over.

"This spring alone over three thousand Chinamen came to Victoria. Three thousand!" Burly shook his head in disgust. "Read it in the *Colonist*. The place is slopping over."

"Slopping over!" Hawk-face slapped the railing to punctuate his laughter. "You sure it's chop suey, not slop chuey?"

Burly smacked him on the back, guffawing at the play on words. "C'mon, let's move to the other side. There's something about the smell around here...."

Jasmine took a deep breath, fighting for control. She wanted to lash out at them, strike them down with the force of her words. But something more than rage smouldered inside.

"I know it hurts," Keung said as the men walked away. "I didn't understand the words, but I understood their meaning."

She swallowed hard. "But why do they talk like that? I don't get it. They don't even *know* us."

"That's why," Keung said. "It's because they don't know us that they do talk like that."

"Why did they call me John?" Jasmine wondered.

"Many whites call us that," Keung replied. "Or Celestial. Or worse." He looked across the water and shook his head sadly. "They don't want us here. In Victoria we can't even work for the city. A friend of Dragon Maker used to light the street lamps on James Bay. He was fired as soon as a white man was found to do the job. No, they don't want us. But they won't have the railway without us. I'm afraid of what will happen when it's finished."

"What will happen? Well, you'll stay. Maybe not *you*, but many Chinese will stay and become teachers and doctors and mayors…."

"And man will walk on the moon," he said bitterly.

Jasmine wanted to shout, *Yes! That will happen too!* But the expression on his face clearly indicated his desire to drop the subject.

The afternoon stretched on as the sternwheeler steamed past the islands that dotted the Gulf of Georgia between Vancouver Island and the mainland. For a long time they stood in silence, watching the pale shades of purple and gold linger on distant hilltops.

By nightfall, the *William Irving* had reached the muddy Fraser. "What place is that?" Jasmine wondered, pointing to a small town rising steeply above the river.

"I think that's Saltwater City. New Westminster, as the barbarians call it." Keung smiled grimly. He was the barbarian now. He knew the whites saw him as an alien, a barbarian without culture, without intelligence, without moral convictions.

"Maybe if you cut your hair and dressed more like white people," Jasmine said. "Maybe it would be easier for you."

"Why? We're not ashamed of who we are. Besides, most of us don't plan to stay here. We only came to make enough money to buy land in China. When we return to our villages we'll still be Chinese. If we cut our hair, we wouldn't be able to return at all."

"What difference does your hair make?"

"When the Manchus conquered China two hundred years ago, they forced men to wear queues, like the long tails of horses. If you didn't wear a queue you'd be put to death. But also, if we cut our hair we are dishonouring our ancestors. Every part of us comes from them."

Jasmine mulled this over. It had never occurred to her that she was a part of something bigger than herself. That so much of what had gone before had led to her.

Later, they crept around the *William Irving,* peering into elegant lounges decorated with tapestries, carpeting, and ornamental woodwork. "Electric lights!" Keung exclaimed, his eyes huge with wonder.

When the night grew cool, they found a sheltered spot near the stern to eat the rice cakes Dragon Maker had provided. A well-dressed Chinese man leaned against the railing, lost in thought. "I recognize him," Keung whispered. "He's a wealthy merchant in Victoria."

A short time later the man approached them. Keung offered his remaining rice cake, and was surprised by the depth of emotion that came over the merchant's face.

"I went to the dining room for dinner," he said, "and sat with the other passengers. The steward ordered me to leave but I refused. For the whole dinner hour I sat there in silence while the waiters ignored me. And you, who have nothing, offer me your rice cake. When you return to Victoria, come and see me. I am Lam Fu Choy." He bowed and wandered off to his cabin.

Except for the swish-swish of the paddlewheel, the night was silent. Jasmine pulled out the quilt Dragon Maker had stuffed in her bag and snuggled underneath. The decking was hard, but no harder than the ground she'd camped out on. Soon she was drifting off, lulled by the gentle motion of the boat.

Keung stared up at the night sky, confused. How could it be the same, so far from home? He could see the Silver River, and the bright stars of Cowherd and Weaving Maid. Here! On the other side of the world!

And this girl! She had pointed to hills even farther west than Victoria. But how could she come from the west, if she was somehow connected to Bright Jade? "Where are you from?" he asked, bewildered.

Jasmine stirred. "Huh? What?" She opened her eyes to find Keung leaning on his elbow, gazing down at her.

"If you're not a spirit, what are you? And who are you? How can you know Bright Jade when you're not one of us? You're a barbarian, in spite of your dark skin and eyes. Even though you speak our language, you're still a barbarian."

"Wait a minute," Jasmine said. "First you wake me up, then you bombard me with questions." She sat up, pulling the quilt tightly around her. "You think I know the answers? I'm as confused as you are. I didn't ask to come into your world. That doorway into Fan Tan Alley? It just happened. I never asked to have the dreams of Bright Jade. They just started, right after my mother died. And I never asked to see you!" She told him about the boy in her dream, how his eyes had locked into hers, how she had recognized him in the gambling den. "Stop staring at me! Can't you see I'm not a spirit?" She took a coin from her shirt pocket and handed it to him. "See the date? This is from my time."

Keung studied the queen on one side, the bird on the other. "But this is over a hundred years away. You *must* be a spirit."

Jasmine touched his hand. "Does this feel like a spirit?"

"No," he said. His face felt hot, and his heartbeat quickened.

"Well then, now we can shake on it."

"Shake on it?"

"It's a saying we have. When two people agree on something, they shake on it. Like this." She took his hand in hers and squeezed it. "You can keep the coin, if you like. It's worth a dollar. We call it a loonie, 'cause the bird's a loon."

"Loon-ie." He repeated the English word and smiled, keeping hold of her hand. Then he said, "I'm sorry about your mother."

"Me too," she said quietly.

For a long time afterward, she could still feel the warmth of his hand. And for the first time since her mother died, she felt less of a piece and more of a whole.

At dawn, the sternwheeler was still steaming up the Fraser. Fir, pine, and spruce loomed on either side of the river. Willows and aspens, their leaves tinged with gold, glowed amongst the evergreens. To Keung, the impenetrable forest and rugged mountains appeared cold and forbidding, a far cry from the warmth of South China.

But to Jasmine, the canyon was electrifying. She clung to the rail, drinking it in. Waterfalls roared down the mountainsides. Creeks flowing into the river were jammed with salmon, making their way to the spawning grounds. Here and there, settlers' cabins appeared on the bank, dwarfed by the hills that towered thousands of feet above the water's edge.

Churning past the town of Hope, the sternwheeler reached Two Sisters, twin rocks where the river dashed and foamed with such ferocity Jasmine could not imagine a boat ever getting through. She felt the steamer tremble, tossed like a cork by the current, while its ponderous wheel continued to revolve under full steam. With a shriek of the whistle it eventually forged ahead, leaving the river lashing into spray against the rocks.

Carefully avoiding driftwood and snags, the *William Irving* continued up the river, through rapids, eddies, and whirlpools. Before long it was steaming around a sharp curve on its final approach to Yale.

From a distance, Yale looked like a sleepy little place, hemmed in by the mountains. But Jasmine's first impression was quickly shattered. Neither she nor Keung were prepared for such a vibrant town. The moment they disembarked they were greeted by a scene of such intensity, colour, and noise, all they could do was stand and gawk.

Crowds of men worked on the beach, handling railway freight and loading it into wagons. The main street fronting the river bustled with activity. People didn't walk, they rushed — people of every shape, size, colour, and costume, from ladies dressed in the latest fashions to Aboriginals carrying freshly speared salmon, speaking every language from Cantonese to Swedish. Horses, mule teams, and oxen kicked up billowing clouds of dust. Dogs ran everywhere.

Front Street was lined with barber shops and blacksmith shops, hotels and general stores, restaurants specializing in fresh oysters and game. The Hudson's Bay Company store advertised wines, liquors, and cigars as well as dry goods and groceries. Shops selling books, fruit, and candies jostled with a meat market, a saddlery, a watch repair shop, even a French bakery. A fleet of freight wagons and stagecoaches waited outside the stables of B.C. Express, and farther down was the Steamboat Exchange. A little ways up the hill stood a church.

And saloons! Every third building seemed to be a saloon. As Keung and Jasmine stood gaping, a couple of men were hurled out of the Gem Saloon and continued their fight on the street. And all the while a wizened old fellow in front of the Cascade House played his concertina.

The noise was deafening. Barks, shouts, cries, and yells competed with the crumps of blasting powder, the rasping of saws, and the hammering of drills and mallets. The screeching of the steamboat whistle added to the din. And the smell! The town reeked of salmon, sawdust, manure, black powder, and tobacco smoke.

Two skippers paused in the dusty street to light their pipes. "Nothing can get through Hell's Gate," Jasmine overheard one skipper say. Her ears pricked up. "That man's a darned fool, make no mistake."

"You gotta give him credit for trying," his companion remarked. "If it works out he'll save a bundle. Freight rates on the Cariboo are costing him plenty."

The first man shook his head. "Might as well jump into Hell's Gate yourself and expect to talk about it."

"So you won't be heading up there?"

"Wouldn't miss it for the world! In fact, I'll lay a little wager. A hundred to one she won't make it."

"Who'd bet in favour of the boat?"

"Oh, there's plenty of fools around, make no mistake." Laughing, the men crossed the road and headed into the Miner's Saloon, leaving Jasmine to wonder what they'd been talking about.

In such a bustling town, two more coolies were scarcely noticed. "We might as well be invisible," Jasmine said. Eyes flicked in her direction from time to time, but dismissed her without a second glance.

"Come on," Keung said. "We'll go to Chinatown and ask about my father."

As they set off, Jasmine had the uneasy feeling that someone had noticed them after all. She turned quickly, just in time to see a man dart behind an ox cart. A man with a scar on his cheek.

Chapter 13

"Do you see him? Right there, behind the ox cart."

Keung looked over his shoulder. There was indeed a scar-faced man, but it wasn't Blue-Scar Wong. "You must be mistaken," he said. "I'm sure he wasn't on the boat. And there's no other way he could have got here so quickly."

"I guess you're right," she said. But the feeling of uneasiness stayed with her, creeping along her veins like the feet of a lizard. Determined to shake it off, she followed Keung into Chinatown.

It was on the eastern side of town. Vertical signs with Chinese characters indicated grocers, laundries, a shoemaker, general stores, and numerous lodging houses. Tantalizing smells of garlic, oyster sauce, and stir-fried chicken spilled from a crowded restaurant on the corner. They entered eagerly and ordered a bowl of noodles topped with slivers of pork, bean sprouts, and crisp celery. Jasmine ate with relish, her earlier fears forgotten.

While they were eating, Keung asked the waiter and other customers about his father. No, they didn't know him. No, they hadn't heard of him. "Many died of scurvy," one man said. "Try Big Mouth Kelly, the man who buries dead Chinese."

"Try Tunnel City," another suggested. "It's where they've been drilling the big tunnel, about twenty miles upriver from Yale. Many camps around there."

"Follow the Wagon Road. But watch out for freight wagons and mule teams. They have to carry everything up the road. Rice for the coolies, even sawmills for construction camps."

"And look out for stagecoaches. They move fast along the road."

After buying some fresh vegetables, they set off along the Cariboo Wagon Road. "This was built in 1862, twenty years ago," said Jasmine. "We learned it in school."

Keung scoffed. "Twenty years? In China our roads are hundreds and hundreds of years old. The Great Wall is over two thousand years old."

"We learned about the Great Wall, too."

Keung's eyes brightened with interest. "You learned about China?"

"Yes, and we went on a field trip to Chinatown

and had Chinese food in a Chinese restaurant. People do that all the time."

"White people, in Chinatown?" He shook his head in disbelief.

The road was jammed with traffic. Double freight wagons drawn by horses rattled over the corduroy road, followed by two ox teams of seven yokes each. Six-mule teams plodded by, pulling covered wagons loaded with supplies. Stagecoaches barrelled through, managing to avoid piles of debris and loose rock.

Like the track bed, the Cariboo Road followed the river. And like the track bed, it was cut into the cliffs, often perilously close to the riverbank. At noon, Jasmine and Keung reached a spot where the road wound around a precipice on trestlework. They crossed over cautiously, trying not to look down at the raging river some two hundred feet below.

Railway crews were everywhere — tunnelling, grading, and blasting, working above the road, beneath the road, and right alongside it. Another explosion rocked the canyon. "I hope we don't get hit," Jasmine said. She covered her ears and glanced around nervously. Steep crags above, roaring river below — not much of a choice if you had to run for it.

Sometimes the road passed so close to the tunnels they could see sparks inside, as steam drills pierced through the flinty rock. At one point, one whole chunk of the road had slid into the Fraser because of the blasting, and crews were hard at work building a new section.

Jasmine shifted her pole to a more comfortable position and strode alongside Keung, easily matching his pace. "What will you do when you find your father?" she asked.

"If we have enough money, return to China."

"That's where my father is right now. Teaching in China."

"These are strange times," he said. "No one's where he's supposed to be."

Jasmine laughed. "Wait till I tell you how he got to China."

"No!" Keung exclaimed after listening to her story. "It can't be true!" He could not imagine a silver tube filled with people flying to the other side of the world. But then, if this person beside him could step through a doorway and journey back in time … and if the spirit of Bright Jade could appear in dreams over a span of two thousand years…. It was too confusing.

Around the next bend they came upon the remains of a tent camp, where a stooped Chinese man scrabbled through the debris looking for food. "Would you like some rice?" Keung asked. "We're about to cook some."

The man accepted gratefully and went off to a nearby stream for water. Keung gathered twigs to start a fire, and in a short time the rice was simmering.

"Fresh vegetables!" The man grinned as Jasmine chopped up some Chinese cabbage. "A change from Siwash chicken."

"Siwash chicken?"

"Dried salmon," he said, grimacing. "Day after day, nothing but Siwash chicken." He tucked into the rice and vegetables, his chopsticks clicking furiously.

"I worked for Lee Chuck Company," he said between mouthfuls, "but no more. Too hard. Now I go back to Saltwater City, maybe get work in a laundry. I've been here since the Year of the Dragon. I was paid eighty cents a day and got my own food. Some made a dollar a day, but had to buy food from company stores at high, high prices." He lowered his voice and glanced around furtively. "You must be careful along these tracks, especially in the tunnels. The ghosts are restless." He shuddered. "My friends were killed in a tunnel up ahead. Smothered to death when the tunnel caved in. No tiger to protect them."

"What do you mean, no tiger?" Keung was instantly alert.

"One of the coolies spoke of a jade amulet with magic powers. But no magic is strong enough here. Not against these mountains."

"Do you know the coolie's name? Or where he is now?"

A glazed look came into the man's eyes. "I don't remember. I don't want to remember."

Keung and Jasmine looked at each other. It must be his father. They were on the right track.

They hiked through the afternoon, spurred on by the feeling that Keung's father was close. As the shadows lengthened and the sun dipped behind the mountains, Keung said, "Let's light a fire and camp here for the night. There's a stream nearby."

Jasmine was only too eager. She was hungry, the bag was heavy, her legs were tired. What's more, the cotton shoes were useless on the rough road. "We'll have to get boots somewhere," she said.

"Tomorrow," Keung agreed as he started a fire.

She chopped bok choy to mix with the rice while Keung sliced thin slivers of ginger. Water bubbled in the kettle for their tea. Slowly, the moon rose over the canyon.

"Do you see the man in the moon?" Jasmine asked.

"Do you see the hare?"

They looked at each other and laughed. "The Moon Lady lives there too," Keung said. "Once she lived on the earth, but then she drank the elixir of life and floated to the moon. Now she lives there forever."

"That's what Bright Jade wanted," Jasmine said, remembering her dream. "Would you like to live forever?"

"Maybe," he replied. "If forever could be like now."

Jasmine smiled. A warm feeling stirred her. What was it — the moon, the stillness of the canyon, the way Keung's face shone in the firelight? Or was it the exhilarating feeling of being, in a sense, free? She didn't know how the magic worked, or how long it would last. But she had consciously, on her own, gone back to the never-ending store to set it in motion. Maybe that was it, the feeling of having some control over her life, at least for this moment.

She placed her chopsticks in the bowl, breathed deeply, and began the tai chi. The patterns came back easily, one flowing into another, one with earth, sky, river, and stars. With each rounded movement of her hands and body she felt the yin and yang, the opposing but harmonious forces in nature. Balance, rhythm, freedom.

In the firelight she could see what appeared to be her shadow, matching every move she made. Then she realized it was Keung. Light and dark, yin and yang. Perfect harmony. Something awoke inside her and sang for joy. And for a second it seemed as though the river stopped rushing, just to listen.

Chapter 14

At first Jasmine thought she was home, in her own bed. But the nightgown she was wearing wasn't hers. And how did her hair get unbraided? Why was her left knee wrapped in a bandage? She touched it gingerly. Ouch! She sat up with a start.

She was in a bedroom, all right, but not her own. Late afternoon sunlight filtered through lace curtains, casting shadows on the pink-flowered wallpaper. An oil lamp with a fluted glass chimney stood on the bedside table. In the corner was a wooden washstand with a jug and a thick china basin, painted with red peonies. A matching chamber pot stood underneath. Where was she? And how did she get here?

Footsteps pattered outside the room, then stopped. A woman popped in, with fluttery hands, a beak of a nose, and beady eyes. "Good gracious girl, you startled me!" she exclaimed, flitting over to draw back the curtains. "Didn't expect to find you awake, but how nice, how nice!" She turned to Jasmine with a broad grin. "We discovered you aren't a boy."

How exactly did you discover that? Jasmine wondered. *And who's we?*

"I'm Nell Jenkins, and you're in my house in Yale. My husband, Harvey, found you, knocked unconscious. Felt your pulse, so he knew you were alive. By the time he brought you in, you were conscious, but in bad shape. Harvey says, 'Nell, put this girl to bed while I fetch the doctor.' So I did, and the doctor came and said there was nothing he could do except bandage up that gash on your knee. So you've been here since yesterday, falling in and out of sleep, and saying some crazy things." She clucked her tongue. "Trains and tigers, jade this, jade that. None of my business, but still."

"Where's Keung?" Jasmine asked. "What happened?"

Mrs. Jenkins didn't seem to hear. "Last night you were there by the fireplace, trying to braid your hair and talking to someone you thought was in the room. I led you back to bed and in a minute you were sound asleep again. But here I am rattling on and you still in a daze. I'll leave you for a bit, get you something to eat. Then we'll see what's to be done." She patted Jasmine on the shoulder. "It's a fine sight to see you awake." With a swish of her long black skirt, she left the room.

Jasmine stepped out of bed, surprised at how wobbly she felt. Her knee ached and her head throbbed. She felt a bump on her temple and winced at the touch. A whole day and night she'd been here? Impossible. But what to do? Find her clothes and get out. That was the first thing. Then find Keung.

She looked at the foot of the bed, under the bed, on the chair, and in the wardrobe. No sign of her clothes anywhere.

Just then Mrs. Jenkins reappeared, carrying a tray. "Here's a bite for you," she said. "Hop back into bed now, there's a girl. Unless you want to use that?" she asked, pointing to the chamber pot.

Jasmine shook her head and dutifully got back into bed. She'd find out about her clothes soon enough. Meanwhile, she was hungry.

"Lord, you gave us quite a scare." Mrs. Jenkins handed Jasmine a cup of tea, then offered her a slice of bread with butter and blueberry preserves. "Take your time," she said. "There's plenty more. Don't suppose you Celestials are used to this kind of food — but then you're not a Celestial, are you?"

Jasmine glanced up quickly.

"I've had a good close look at you, my dear." Her hands, never still, flicked through her hair and picked imaginary lint off her sleeves. "You're as white as I am, though your eyes are awfully dark. Wouldn't have guessed it at first, what with the clothes you were wearing. Though why you were hiking along the road dressed like a coolie is none of my business. You running away from something, maybe? You're lucky you weren't hurt by worse than flying rock. This is no place for a young girl to be roaming around. What's your name, by the way?"

"Jasmine."

"Pretty name, that. Like the flower. Where you from?"

"Victoria." Close enough to the truth.

"Your folks in Victoria?"

"I'm staying with my aunt. My mother's dead and my father's in China."

Mrs. Jenkins slapped her knee. "Well, if that don't beat all. Some kind of mission worker, is he?"

Jasmine ignored the question. "How did I get here, Mrs. Jenkins? What happened?"

"Harvey found you. Came round the bend on the Cariboo Road right after the explosion. He drives the stagecoach, you see. Lord, if he'd been any faster he'd have been caught, same as you."

"Explosion?" The word brought back a sudden flash. A blast that shook the ground, smoke, then another blast, rocks hurtling down the mountainside, screams….

Mrs. Jenkins nodded. "They're blasting north of Spuzzum. Lord, they're always blasting somewheres. In Yale here, we had to put up with that shaking for months. Twenty-four hours a day, rock blown to bits, but not a single piece of track laid. Drilling the tunnels first, you see.

"Well, just before Harvey comes along, they're blasting this half-finished tunnel. Too much powder I guess, though there's always something going wrong. Anyways, there's a blast and the coolies start heading back in. Then there's a second blast. They're blown to pieces. Rocks falling all over the road."

She clucked her tongue, gave a quick shake of her head. "Rock slides happening all the time. And rocks shooting out of tunnels. One landed in the river, sank a boat. Another one knocked down a bridge. You sure were lucky. Lord, there's been so many accidents...."

Jasmine twisted a strand of hair tightly around her finger. Bit by bit, it was coming back — hiking along the Cariboo Road, camping by the stream, setting off the next morning. And Keung's voice. "There's another explosion. Hear it?"

Jasmine listened to the crump of explosives. "Is it safe to be on the road?" she asked.

"Safe as anywhere else," he replied.

Up ahead they could hear the steam drills as another gang prepared to blast through the granite. Then it came. A burst of fire and smoke, the boom of the explosion rolling along the narrow gorge. Jasmine trembled as the ground shook beneath her feet. "I hope that's the end of it for a while," she said.

When they reached the half-finished tunnel, men were already back inside. "That must be the worst —"

"Get down!" Keung's scream was sudden and unexpected. With one swift motion he knocked her down and threw himself across her body.

She hit the ground hard, face pressed into the dirt. Felt something sharp dig into her knee. Breathed in dust, smoke, the acrid smell of powder. Heard screams, a rumble of boulders. Felt a blow on her head, shards of stabbing pain. Then silence.

"Keung?" She could no longer feel his body. From a great distance she heard, *Jasmine, run!* She struggled to get up. But darkness pressed down, the earth opened up and swallowed her in.

Mrs. Jenkins was rambling on, "…thought he was perfectly safe, hiding behind a tree. Long ways from the tunnel, or so he thought. Poor man lost his nose. Sliced right off!"

"What happened to Keung?" Jasmine burst out. "The Chinese boy who was with me, he saved my life! Your husband must have seen him!"

"There, there," said Mrs. Jenkins, patting her on the head. "*You* were lucky you made it alive."

"But he *has* to be all right. Someone must have seen him."

"Dear girl, you were the only one found alive. Could be that boy got buried."

"No!" She fought the tightening in her chest, telling herself not to panic.

Mrs. Jenkins brushed a few stray crumbs from her blouse. "Good gracious, why such a fuss about a coolie? Another one'll come to take his place. He was just another —"

"No, he wasn't! You wouldn't say that if —"

"Now, now, don't get yourself excited." Mrs. Jenkins picked up the tray and left the room.

Sometime later, Jasmine appeared in the kitchen. "Could I please have my clothes?" she asked.

"If you mean those filthy coolie rags, certainly not," Mrs. Jenkins said indignantly. "Whatever you were doing in that get-up is none of my business, though I am mighty curious. But come on, I got something real nice for you to wear."

She ushered Jasmine back to the bedroom, opened a dresser drawer, and handed her a petticoat and a pair of bloomers. Then she reached into the wardrobe and took out a pale blue dress flecked with pink flowers. "This belonged to my daughter when she was about your age."

Jasmine ignored the dress. "You've been really kind and I appreciate it, but I need my own clothes. And what happened to my bag? The cotton bag on the bamboo pole?"

"There wasn't a bag. You know, last night you were rambling something strange. Maybe your head still isn't right. You were hit by an awful big rock." She nodded with satisfaction. "That could explain things. You're still not quite yourself."

"I need my clothes!"

"Put these on for now." Before Jasmine could protest further, the woman had whisked away.

Well, at least I'll get this thing off, she thought as she threw the scratchy nightgown over her head. She slipped on the bloomers and petticoat, then the dress.

As she was fastening it up, Mrs. Jenkins returned with a pair of high buttoned boots. "Try these on." She smiled as Jasmine pulled them on. "My, don't you look a picture. Wouldn't know you're the same girl Harvey brought in."

"I'm not," Jasmine mumbled.

"Oh, go on with you. Now tomorrow, the doctor's taking the sternwheeler to Victoria and he's agreed to take you with him."

Jasmine looked up sharply. "But —"

"No buts, now," Mrs. Jenkins said with a wave of her hands. "It's all arranged. The doctor's even paying your way. Now I've got an errand for you. If you're feeling up to it?"

Jasmine nodded. If Mrs. Jenkins gave her an errand in town, maybe she'd learn what happened to Keung.

"You can go to the grocer's, then help with supper. Water in that jug should still be warm enough for washing, and the outhouse is out back. I'll be in the kitchen if you need me."

Jasmine spotted her clothes on the way back from the outhouse — a dark pile stashed behind the woodshed. Pants, jacket, shoes, hat, even her underwear and shirt, with the $20 bill her aunt had given her tucked inside the pocket. Everything was there, except for the bag.

Gathering up the bundle, she crept past the kitchen, along the hall, and into the bedroom. She poured water into the basin, washed the clothes as best she could, and hung them in the wardrobe to dry. She was throwing the dirty water out the window when Mrs. Jenkins stepped in. "Thought I heard you. Had a good wash, did you?"

"Yes, thanks," she said with a pleased grin.

Mrs. Jenkins handed her a coin. "If you fetch me some fresh eggs from McKay's we'll be all set. He's down the hill, on the corner."

"But this is only twenty-five cents."

"Go on with you, girl. Two bits is more than enough for a dozen eggs. Just make sure you don't go all the way into town. It's much too rowdy for a girl on her own."

Chapter 15

One dozen eggs. *Pretty basic,* Jasmine thought as she walked past McKay's. She had no intention of going to the main part of town, only to the Chinese part. She could just as easily get eggs there. And information.

She hadn't anticipated the stares. Eyes followed her down the street, men stopped in their tracks to gape. A young white girl, alone, in Chinatown. So much for the invisible stranger. Never before had she felt so conspicuous. *It's this stupid dress,* she thought angrily. Dragging down her confidence. Waving her out like a banner.

But she'd always taken pride in being different, in being uniquely herself. So. She hitched up the skirt, straightened her shoulders, and carried on, ignoring the stares. But now her knee was starting to hurt. "Great," she muttered as she limped along. Past the restaurant where she and Keung had eaten, past a laundry, until she reached a general store.

Perfect. She could buy boots as well as eggs. She crossed the small verandah and entered the wooden building. Long counters extended along each side, with shelves reaching to the ceiling. The right side held groceries, the left side dry goods and hardware, boots and shoes. A small shelf held an altar with sticks of burning incense. At the back, a group of men stood chatting around a large wood stove.

Boldly, she stepped up to the counter. "I'm wondering if you know anything about the explosion yesterday, or if you've seen a Chinese boy, about my age, whose name is Chan Tai Keung. And I'd like some eggs, please. And a pair of boots, for me."

A sudden silence crushed in around her. The men by the stove gawked. The clerk stared, bewildered. When she held out the green $20 bill with Queen Elizabeth's picture on the back, he shook his head firmly and pointed to the door. Undeterred, Jasmine walked over to the boots and picked up a pair. "These look sturdy enough. Do you have my —"

Abruptly, she stopped. She'd spoken in English. The clerk was speaking a Chinese dialect but she could not understand a single word.

With burning cheeks she scuttled out of the store, the bill crumpled in her hand. *Stupid!* Of course they wouldn't think this was real money. But why couldn't she speak their language?

Her throat swelled with tears of humiliation and frustration. Stupid! And what about Keung? How could she ever find him if she'd lost the language? What a mess! And she still didn't have the wretched eggs.

She limped off to McKay's, wincing at the pain in her knee, cursing the ridiculous skirt and the high boots that pinched her toes. Her head throbbed with every step.

"And where might you be from?" Mr. McKay asked as he handed her the eggs.

She turned away, flustered. Everything was in such a muddle she hardly knew anymore. And she certainly didn't want to talk about it. In her eagerness to leave, she moved too quickly, tripped over the skirt, and fell to the floor.

As the grocer was helping her up, a thought struck her. "Of course!" she exclaimed. "It's something to do with the clothes!" She grinned at the astonished Mr. McKay and hurried out the door.

"Now there be a strange one," he said, watching her stumble up the hill. "At least she didn't break the eggs."

Harvey Jenkins finished carving the roast and turned to the newspaper while his wife heaped servings of string beans, carrots, and mashed pota-toes on the plates. "*Here in British Columbia along the line of the railway,*" he read aloud, "*the China workmen are fast disappearing under the ground.*" He put down the *Yale Sentinel* and dove into his dinner. "In just one week, six died outta twenty-eight down below Emory," he said in a booming voice. "That's almost one outta four."

Mrs. Jenkins clucked her tongue. "More than that died of scurvy, right here in Yale. Remember, Harvey? We were so scared it was smallpox." She tucked into her food. "C'mon girl, eat. That's fresh venison. And the vegetables are from our own garden."

Jasmine forced down a few mouthfuls.

"Y'know," Mr. Jenkins said, "coolies have a funny attitude toward death. When one of them gets sick with scurvy, the others just let him be. Lose interest altogether."

"A friend of mine picked up a deserted coolie once," said Mrs. Jenkins. "Found him by the side of the road, took him into her own home, and nursed him back to health. Can you imagine? Anyways, when he was better she took him back to camp. But the coolies thought he was a ghost, and Lord, did they ever hightail it out of there!" She laughed and helped herself to more gravy. "Took them some time before they believed he was really alive."

"I think they believe it's bad luck," Jasmine said. "To work where there's been a death."

"Well then, it's a wonder they're still around." Mr. Jenkins wiped his bristly moustache and loaded his plate with more food. "There's hardly a stretch of this canyon that hasn't seen a Chinese death of one kind or other."

He paused long enough to wolf down his second helping. "But one thing you got to admit. They sure can work. Listen to this." He picked up the newspaper and read: "*In July 1882 without a horse or cart or steam 1,031 Chinese using only picks, shovels, drills, and wheelbarrows excavated 88,147 yards of earth, 10,081 yards of loose rock, and 16,462 yards of solid rock. These men landed in Victoria three months before and had to be taught how to hold a shovel and strike a drill, some of them ascending cliffs 200 feet high with the aid of ropes to reach their work, clinging to rocks with foaming rivers beneath.*" He put down the paper, gave his moustache a tug. "Better them than me, that's all I can say."

"Enough of this talk, now," Mrs. Jenkins said. "Lord, girl, you eat like a grasshopper. What's your favourite food in Victoria? Surely you eat more than this."

"I love lasagna," Jasmine said. "And raspberry mousse for dessert."

The Jenkins raised their eyebrows. "Never heard of that," Mr. Jenkins said. "Mind you, we got plenty of moose. Never seen a raspberry moose, though. That would be a sight."

"You'll eat some of my dessert, won't you?" Mrs. Jenkins asked. "Don't know anything about your mousse, but the most healthy dessert that can be placed on the table is a baked apple. The newspaper itself said so."

"Hogwash," Mr. Jenkins bellowed as he poured custard over the apple. "Forget the *Sentinel* and go back to making pies."

Mrs. Jenkins ignored her husband. "You must be excited about heading home tomorrow, Jasmine. Your aunt will be tickled pink. But it's a shame you'll miss the *Skuzzy*. That's going to be something to see."

"Yessir," Mr. Jenkins agreed. "Onderdonk's gonna get a steamboat through Hell's Gate if it kills him."

"Who's Onderdonk?" Jasmine asked.

"Why, he's the head boss around here, the one that's building the railway through the canyon. He's the one brought all them Chinese to do it."

"Hell's Gate … is it far from here?"

"About twenty miles, isn't it, Harvey? But tell us, Jasmine. Tell us all about Victoria." Mrs. Jenkins leaned forward eagerly.

Jasmine pushed the unfinished apple to another spot on her plate. *Which one?* she wondered.

The Victoria now, or later? "Well," she began, "my aunt lives in a condominium on the water-front, on the ninth floor. At night I can see the Legislative Buildings all lit up, and the Empress Hotel — that's a famous CPR hotel. It's built on mudflats and a bay that got filled in a long time ago. I mean, a few years from now. Right now there's ..."

Her voice trailed off. She twisted a strand of hair, every bit as confused as the Jenkins. How to explain it? Better stick to her time. "I'm staying with my aunt 'cause Dad flew to China last week in a 747, a big jet. I'm going to meet him there. It's a long flight though, thirteen hours, and you lose a day, so if I leave on a Monday, I get to China on Wednesday. Tuesday's just gone. But you get an extra day when you come back to the west."

The Jenkins stared at her, dumbfounded.

"I don't understand it either," she said. "Time and travel, I mean."

"Poor dear child." Mrs. Jenkins' hands fluttered over to Jasmine and stroked her head. "You *have* been hurt in that explosion. Such talk, such foolishness. Imagine, anyone flying to China."

"It's true. When I get back I'll send you a postcard of a 747 and one of the Empress —" No she wouldn't. How could she? By the time she got back, in *that* time, the Jenkins would be gone.

"Oh, just send a postcard of the Birdcages. That would be nice, just to let us know you've arrived home safely."

"Thank you," Jasmine said quietly. "For dinner and for taking me in. I'm fine now, really. I'll be all right."

It was dark when she finally went to her room. Automatically, she reached for the light switch. Then remembered. She lit the oil lamp and carefully turned down the wick. In the glow of lamplight she put on the coolie clothes. So what if they still smelled of powder and smoke. They were clean, they were dry, and they clung to her like an old friend. She braided her hair and tied it with a leather thong. Now she was ready. All she needed was a few hours sleep.

Sometime later she was wakened by a faint scratching sound, like leaves brushing against the windowpane. *Scrrritch*. But it wasn't leaves. A chill crept into her. What was it? The fingernails of Blue-Scar Wong? Claws, scraping down the glass? Her heart beat faster. She stole to the window and pushed the curtains aside.

A shape spun out of the moonlight, luminous and white. Its yellow eyes pierced deep inside her. A huge paw stretched toward her. Then froze. She felt its power in the rippling of muscles beneath the skin. Felt its magic. *Stay,* she breathed. *Tell me where he is.*

The tiger threw back its head and roared. Through the yard, through the town, through the canyon, the sound echoed from crag to crag, from tunnel to tunnel, from camp to camp, like a long roll of thunder.

As the echoes died, the tiger drifted away until its shape was nothing more than a fading dream. But its message was clear. The white jade tiger was awake, and waiting to be found.

Jasmine was up before daybreak. She opened the window, swung over the sill, and dropped the short distance to the ground. She stole through the garden, unlatched the gate, and shut it behind her. Then she flew down the hill, her dark clothes blending with the shadows, her heart pounding with excitement. When she reached the tracks she turned and followed the rails out of Yale, north toward Hell's Gate.

It wasn't long before her exhilaration gave way to more practical concerns. She still needed boots. And what happened to her bag? What would she do at night without the quilt? What would she do about food? Her money was useless. Would she have to scrounge through garbage? Or start begging?

Her worries were interrupted by voices coming from behind. A gang of Chinese coolies — and this time, she could understand their language. "Did you hear about the explosion?" she asked. "A couple of days ago?"

"Oh, yes," they replied. "Rocks flying everywhere. Many were killed." But no, they hadn't heard of anyone buried on the road.

"Where are you going now?" The coolies were loaded down with all their belongings, provisions, and camp equipment.

"To another camp, on the other side of the Big Tunnel."

"Is that near Hell's Gate?"

"Between Hell's Gate and Spuzzum. Lots of people going there today. All the way from Yale, to see a boat go through the rapids." They shook their heads and laughed. "A boat through Hell's Gate? A crazy idea! Impossible!"

Before long, Jasmine had outpaced the coolies and left them far behind. Gradually, the sky grew lighter. Sunlight streaked along the rails, turning the steel into shiny metallic threads.

A ringing bell and a rattling over the newly laid track broke the morning stillness. Round the bend it came, a locomotive pushing five flat cars loaded with men, women, and children polished up in their Sunday best.

"Hey, John!" one youth shouted. "We're off to see the *Skuzzy*. Wanna ride? Toss up a pigtail and we'll haul …" Jasmine lost his words as the train plunged into a tunnel.

Skuzzy. She remembered. The boat that was going through Hell's Gate.

The ragged mouth of the tunnel gaped open. She gulped. *Just do it,* her inner voice urged. *You've already been through three this morning. So what if this is the longest? So what if it's the darkest?* She tried to ignore the clammy feel of the air, the weight of the mountain pressing in on her, the steady drip, drip of water falling from the jagged rock above her head. *Come on. One step at a time, toward the light.* Finally, she was back in the sunshine.

Mile after mile she trudged. Stopping at streams to drink icy water and splash it on her face. Through the Big Tunnel, three times as long as any of the others. Over trestles, spanning creeks and gullies. Stopping for blackberries to ease the pangs of hunger. At least her knee wasn't aching.

After braving three more tunnels, she stumbled into an excited crowd of people stretched out along the riverbank, high above the Fraser. Cautiously, she stepped to the edge, looked down, and gasped.

This was it, the place from her dream. *Déjà vu* — the river raging over ledges of rock, squeezing between twin towers of granite; the narrow opening, boiling with spray. If she squinted her eyes, stared hard, maybe the image of Bright Jade would appear.

"Welcome to Hell's Gate, John. Stick around, you might see history made."

Jasmine turned to the stout, bushy-haired man beside her. "See that?" He pointed to a steamboat struggling in the rapids. The rush of water was so great the boat was smashed against one side then thrown with a grinding crash against the other. "That's the *Skuzzy*. They're going to move her up through Hell's Gate as far as Lytton. Harebrained scheme of Mr. Onderdonk, the railway contractor. But I guess you know all about him."

Jasmine wasn't sure whether the man knew if she could understand or not. It didn't seem to matter, for after taking a long draw on his pipe he continued. "One hundred twenty-seven feet long, she is. Two hundred fifty tons. Launched in May by Mrs. Onderdonk herself. First skipper that's asked to bring her through says no. So another skipper's found and by this time, the river's rising higher and higher. Spring flow, you see. Well this skipper tries and tries, but the river wins every time. Finally, he gives up. So what does Onderdonk do?

Finds some more fools to try again. One of these skippers has actually taken a boat over the falls on the Snake River, down in Oregon."

He paused to blow a trail of smoke rings. "Onderdonk must think it's going to work this time. Why else would he bring all these folks up special to watch the performance? I dunno," he said. "Don't hold your breath on this one, John." He sauntered off, sucking on his pipe and muttering to himself.

Jasmine paced along the bank, searching for some sign of a camp. All around her, men were laying bets on the outcome of the *Skuzzy*'s struggle — wagers of gold, timber, anything — all against the boat. Seeing the pitiful headway it was making, Jasmine would have bet against its chances, too.

What about her chances? She would bet one hundred to one Keung was somewhere near Hell's Gate. Maybe in that camp farther ahead, where smoke was rising above the trees. She headed toward it, hoping it was a Chinese tent camp, hoping she wouldn't have to go any farther.

The chatter of voices told her she was partly right. She stopped the first coolie she came to. "Chan Tai Keung?" She was too tired to say anything more.

The coolie repeated the name. "Young? Same height as you?"

"Yes, yes! Where is he?"

The man pointed to a sagging gray tent at the far end of the camp. "The last time I saw him he was in there. But I don't think —"

Jasmine didn't wait to hear the rest. She rushed toward the tent, giddy with relief. Without thinking, she pushed open the flap and burst in.

Chapter 16

The smell hit her with such force she thought she would be sick. She sank against the tent wall, fighting back the nausea, the need to get outside. *Hang on,* she told herself. *Wait till your eyes are used to the dark. Wait to see if he's here.*

It was stifling inside the tent. The air was thick and oppressive, heavy with the silence of opium dreams. Shadowy figures lay still as death, packed in rows upon straw mattresses spread over the dirt floor.

A man sat at a plank table, preparing the pipes. Jasmine watched with a mixture of fascination and repugnance. First, he dipped a long needle into a tin. Then he held it up, twirling until the sticky black stuff formed a bead-like pellet. Carefully, he held the pellet over the lamp to heat it. Then he put it into a long-stemmed pipe and handed it to one of the men.

They look like ghosts, Jasmine thought, scanning their faces. *More ghostly than any I've seen in my dreams.* She watched as one ghost took the pipe and sucked the vapour deeply into his lungs. It seemed as though he held it there forever. Finally he released it, filling the air with another long plume of smoke. He was about to lie back when his eyes drifted over to Jasmine.

"Keung," she breathed. In spite of the dim light there was no mistake.

He did not respond. With a euphoric smile, he floated back to his dreams.

She stepped over bodies and around mattresses to get close to him. "Keung," she whispered urgently. "Wake up. Please."

The opium man approached her. "It's no use," he said. "You'll have to wait until that pellet wears off. Would you like some? One dollar a pipe."

She shook her head, feeling the sting of tears and the warning heave of her stomach. She stumbled outside and retched violently, over and over again.

A short time later, she spotted a vegetable garden at the edge of the camp. A stream flowed alongside. She staggered toward it and splashed water over her face. Then she returned to the opium tent and sat outside to wait. One hour? Two? It didn't matter.

Sometime later, she felt a hand on her shoulder, gently shaking her awake. "Keung!" Her throat swelled with tears. "What happened to you? They told me you were buried in the explosion. I was so afraid."

He patted her arm. "Are you hungry? Come on."

His camp was close to the stream and garden, away from the cluster of tents. "The stagecoach driver found me," Jasmine explained as Keung lit a fire and put on the rice. "He took me to Yale and I had to wear an ugly dress because his wife threw away my clothes, and I went to Chinatown…." Bit by bit the story came out, right down to her vision of the tiger.

When the meal was ready, Keung handed her a cotton bag on a bamboo pole. "I kept this for you."

She stifled a desire to hug him. "Thank goodness!" She fished out her bowl and chopsticks and gulped down the food. Nothing had ever tasted so good.

"I remember hearing the blast and throwing you down," said Keung. "Then I was hit by a falling rock. When I came to, you were gone. All that was left was the bag. I thought you had vanished, like before. So I joined a gang heading north."

"But why the opium?"

"I hoped you would come back in a dream."

"And did I?"

He paused before answering. "Yes, but in a different way. And in a different time."

"I am from a different time."

"Yes, but …" He shrugged his shoulders, unable or unwilling to explain. "It was only an opium dream."

"And your father?"

"Still nothing. But I'm sure he's close."

Throughout the camp, fires crackled and hissed. Night closed in with the smells of cooking and the sounds of tired voices.

"I signed on," Keung said. "So I can earn money to return to China."

"Then I'll sign on too. How do I do it?"

"You can't do this work!" Keung protested. "It's ridiculous."

"No more ridiculous than me coming here in the first place. No one even looks at me. I'm dressed like all the coolies, I'm as tall as you and I'm really strong." *And flat-chested*, she added silently. "I'll keep my face hidden and my mouth shut. Just say I'm your cousin and make up a name."

Keung sighed. There was no arguing with her. Dragon Maker was right, she had a fiery spirit. "All right," he said. And realized with a start that he was proud of her.

"I need boots like yours," she said, eyeing his sturdy work boots.

His dimples flashed in a warm smile. "Tomorrow I'll take you to the bookman and get you the boots."

"You want eighty cents a day or a dollar?" the book-man asked.

Jasmine thought. If she took a dollar she'd have to buy all her supplies at the company stores, at high prices. But she didn't expect to stay long, so how many supplies would she need? She held up one finger.

"Dollar it is," he said. "But if you buy something from another store, you're discharged immediately. And whenever we move, you pack all your belongings and set up your own camp."

"A dollar a day isn't much," Jasmine said as they hiked to the worksite.

Keung looked at her with surprise. "It's less than a white man makes, but it's a fortune compared to China. There, a peasant only makes seven cents a day."

"Seven cents?" Jasmine gasped. "Everyone who works here must go home rich!"

"That's what I thought, too," he said. "But the men who were hired before leaving China have to pay back the cost of their passage. So every month there's money taken away for that. And every month they send money home to support their families. Many thought they could save enough to buy land. Now they know it's just a dream."

An hour later they reached the worksite. A tunnel was being dug into the mountain. Near the roof of the tunnel, a gang of Chinese coolies was already at work. On galleried platforms at several different levels they drilled blasting holes, inserted the dynamite, lit the fuses, and ran for cover. When the explosion settled, a gang armed with pickaxes smashed the rock into chunks and removed the debris.

Outside the tunnel, more rock had been drilled and blasted, then broken into fragments to fill up the roadbed. "That's our job," Keung said, handing Jasmine a shovel. "Load the loose rock into a wheelbarrow and dump it into the cuts and hollows. Once the roadbed's finished, the tracks are laid."

Pile after pile of shattered rock had to be moved. Soon every muscle in her body was screaming. And she'd thought digging the garden was back-breaking work. Bend, lift, bend, lift. Her body was one long, deep groan. And this had been her idea? Mrs. Jenkins was right. Something must have happened to her head.

After forever, the straw boss told them they could stop for tea. "Is it quitting time?" she asked, collapsing in a heap beside Keung. She hardly had the energy to lift her cup.

He laughed. "It's only been three hours! There's seven more to go."

At the halfway mark they stopped for a meal of dried salmon and rice. The coolies grumbled about the Siwash chicken while their huge tea kettles simmered over fires all along the line.

Bend, lift, heave, groan. She shovelled smaller loads now, hoping no one would notice. She moved more slowly, cursing the new boots and the blisters on her feet. She wished the day would end. She wished the tiger would come and spirit her away.

Every so often a warning shot would go off and everyone would run out of the tunnel to escape the blast. Inch by inch they were drilling their way through the mountain, although the granite wall seemed endless and their progress unbelievably slow.

She pitied the men inside the tunnel. All day long, breathing in loose dirt, their eyes stinging from the fumes of blasting powder. A whole mountain looming above their heads. One fuse improperly lit, one moment's hesitation…. She filled her lungs with cool, fresh air, thankful she wasn't hidden from the light and sky.

Bend, lift, heave, groan. *Hey, Dad, remember how you used to say I wasn't afraid of hard work? Well, guess what I've been doing? Building the railway for the CPR, that's what, with the Chinese coolies. Yes, really. Who me, delirious? Not a chance. Yes, I'd like to take a train trip through the Fraser Canyon when I get back to my time. No, I don't know how long I'll be. However long it takes, I guess, unless Bright Jade and the tiger have other ideas. Bright Jade and the tiger? You mean I haven't told you? Well …*

The day was over. They trudged back. No one spoke.

After the first few days, her muscles stopped aching.

Or had she stopped feeling altogether? A numbness had set in. Eventually the monotonous grind of work would end, but she didn't know when. Or how.

Meanwhile, the *Skuzzy* was still trying to get through Hell's Gate. After four days, the crowds from Yale had returned home. It was obvious the *Skuzzy* was getting nowhere. Eight days later, the situation was the same. After ten days, Onderdonk made a decision.

"What are all those herders doing here?" Jasmine wondered as several white bosses rushed into their camp. "What's happening?"

The bosses began rounding up the coolies. "Let's go, John. Big job, very important." They herded them to the riverbank where coolies were lining up on both sides of the canyon.

"There must be a hundred and fifty here," Jasmine said. "What's going on?"

Keung could only shrug. Whatever it was, it wouldn't be easy. Otherwise, why would they have rounded up 150 Chinese? And what were the thick ropes for, twisting along the banks?

"Oh god," said Jasmine, pointing to the *Skuzzy*. A dozen men were securing the ends of ropes around the ship's capstan. "I think we have to pull it through the rapids."

She was right. Ring bolts had been driven into the rock walls of the canyon. The heavy ropes passed through the hands of the coolies, through the bolts and down to the *Skuzzy*.

She closed her eyes and tried not to think of the river raging below. To make matters worse, a steady rain had started to fall. One faltering grip, one false step on the slippery ground, meant certain death. She dug in the heels of her cotton shoes, wishing she'd had time to change into the boots.

The rope was slick with sweat and grime. She grasped it as tightly as she could, loathing the feel of it, like the knotted sinews of some horrible monster that would squeeze the life right out of her.

"Pull!"

She pulled until her arms ached, pulled until her stomach coiled in knots as twisted as the strands of rope. Through the rain and wind-whipped spray she could see the steam pouring from the *Skuzzy*'s smokestack, the boilers close to bursting.

As she strained and pulled, she could hear the groans of the others, feel them seeping inside. Or were they the groans of the ghosts, returning from her dream? What did it matter? They might as well all be ghosts. "Pull!" the herders shouted.

As if we weren't already pulling our guts out, she thought. *What do they think? That we want to let go and fall into Hell's Gate with their stupid* Skuzzy?

Anger made her pull harder. Her mind blocked out everything but the feel of the rope burning in her hands. After a while, it seemed as though a darkness came over her. Not the terrifying darkness of the tunnel, but a welcoming darkness, lit by the dream ghosts, urging her on.

Later, she sat by the campfire, nursing her sore hands, too exhausted to move. "The amazing thing is," she said, "we actually did it. We pulled the boat through."

"They're having a holiday in Yale to celebrate," said Keung.

"How about here?"

He gave a bitter laugh. "Not for the coolies."

In the stillness just before dawn the opium man crept over and shook Keung awake. "Someone is looking for you and your cousin," he whispered. "A man in a long robe. A wealthy merchant."

Keung shot up. "Does he have a scar on his face?"

The man nodded.

"What did you tell him? Where is he now?"

"In the opium tent. I said I haven't seen you, but others may tell a different story. He's asking about your father, too. Do you know this man? What does he want with you?"

"I can't explain now. Jasmine, wake up. We have to leave quickly."

"Where are you going?" the man asked. "What should I tell him?"

"Tell him we've gone back to Victoria," Jasmine said. Shakily, she packed their belongings while Keung went to collect their pay. Her mouth felt dry, her legs weak and watery. Blue-Scar Wong had found them.

Chapter 17

They headed north as the light of a chill autumn morning filtered through the canyon. "If Blue-Scar's in the opium tent, he'll be there for a while," Keung said. "Even if he doesn't believe we've gone to Victoria, we'll have a head start."

"How far are we going?" Jasmine wondered.

"As far as it takes. We've got to find my father, especially now that Blue-Scar is here. We'll try every camp along the way. What else can we do? He isn't in Yale, he isn't in Spuzzum. Maybe Boston Bar. Maybe Lytton."

"Did the bookman pay you?"

Keung grinned. "Yes, although he grumbled when I woke him up so early. But he was too sleepy to ask any questions. Here. I've counted out your share."

"Keep it. What would I do with it anyway? It's as useless in my time as my five-dollar bill is in yours."

"But you'll need it for the boat, if you go back to Victoria without me."

"There's no way I'm going back without you," she said, her mouth set in a determined line.

She shivered as they strode along, hoping they would find Chan Sam before it got much colder. On the mountainsides, above the splashes of red and yellow, she could see the snow line creeping lower and lower.

A sudden thought snapped in her mind, a thought she hadn't considered. What if she were still here in winter? What then? It was already the end of September. She had assumed that once they found the white jade tiger she would be whisked back to her own time. Her stomach twisted sharply, as if she'd just swallowed a splinter of glass. What if it didn't work that way? What if she were stuck here and couldn't get back?

A tunnel brought her sharply back to the present. *One step at a time,* she told herself. *Worry about the rest later. Or don't worry. Just wait and see.* She took a deep breath and plunged inside.

"Do you feel the ghosts?" Keung whispered. "They're restless because they haven't been properly buried. All Chinese want to be buried with their ancestors. Then their spirits can be at peace. In Victoria, their bones are dug out of the graveyard after seven years and shipped back to China."

Jasmine grimaced. "That's awful!"

"After seven years the body is decomposed," Keung continued. "It's bones, nothing more. And the spirit is happy to be going home. Would you like to stay forever in a foreign land that didn't want you?"

"No." She couldn't imagine being dead, let alone unhappy with her burial place. All she wanted was to get out of the tunnel. And as for being in a foreign land, she *was*, wasn't she? Or might as well be. A pattering sound made her heart beat faster. Footsteps pursuing her in the dark? No. Only water dripping from the ceiling. "Why are the Chinese so concerned with the dead?" she asked.

"We gain strength from our ancestors," Keung explained. "And hope they will be proud of us."

She quickened her step as they neared the end of the tunnel. "Your ancestors must be proud of you," she said. "You were brave to come all this way by yourself, especially since you're so young. And brave to go looking for your father."

Keung smiled. "I'm not so young. I'm sixteen, and a Tiger Boy. People born in the Year of the Tiger are supposed to be fearless, courageous, and powerful. But sometimes I haven't felt very brave. Tiger people also think too deeply and are too sensitive. But they can be quick-tempered and fierce like a tiger." He roared playfully as they burst into the light.

Jasmine laughed. "I'm a Dragon Girl. I'm sensitive and quick-tempered, too. Energetic and stubborn."

"Dragon people are also very brave. I'm sure your ancestors will be proud of you. You've come a great distance too, but in a different way."

"I hope they'll be proud of me." It suddenly struck her that she knew very little about her ancestors. A bit about her grandparents, although they had died before she was born. But before that? It wasn't something her parents had talked about. And she'd never thought to ask. "I wish I knew who my ancestors were," she said.

"Perhaps you'll discover them one day. If you keep travelling back in time, you may even meet them."

She smiled happily, pleased with the thought.

A bridge stretched before them, high above the creek. Jasmine groaned. If it wasn't a tunnel, it was a trestle bridge. She gritted her teeth and took a step forward. She was a Dragon Girl, after all. Somewhere, her unknown ancestors were watching.

"Don't look down," Keung said. "Keep looking ahead, at the gang working on the other side. See, they're laying ties and rails."

She concentrated on the sounds of hammering and tried to ignore the creaking of timbers beneath her feet. *It's perfectly safe,* she told herself, glancing at the piers of solid masonry supporting the spans. *It's built to carry a train. Even if it's over a hundred feet high, it's perfectly safe. One step at a time. Over the first span.* At least she was in the open, not inside a tunnel. But which was worse? She remembered a discussion she'd had with Krista. *Would you rather be too cold or too hot? Too cold. No, wait — too hot. No, too cold…. Stop it. There, over the second span. What if a train should come? Walk faster. Would you rather fall from a trestle or be buried in a tunnel? Faster. Faster.*

"I did it!" she exclaimed. "Way faster, this time."

The wind picked up as the day wore on, and dark clouds threatened rain. They passed several camps, some with tents, some with crude log cabins. Gangs of coolies laboured everywhere. But there was no sign of Chan Sam.

At China Bar they met a man panning for gold. "The whites left, so I took over the claim. I've been lucky." He smiled broadly.

"Did you work on the railway?" Keung asked.

"For a while I worked on the cliffs. They lowered me down on ropes and I drilled holes in the rock walls for explosives. Then they pulled me up before the blast. When the rock was blown away there was a foothold so other men could stand and work." He looked up at the rugged peaks. "With nothing but shovels we changed the shape of these mountains. But the mountain spirits kept many of us in payment. Now I find gold. It pays better, if you're lucky. Sometimes I find jade in the river. Always green though, never white."

"Have you heard of the white jade tiger?"

His eyes widened. "You speak of this too? Not long ago a merchant came by, asking about this tiger. But no, I know nothing."

The bridge at Skuzzy Creek looked even more nerve-rattling than the one before, especially with the wind whipping across it. "Why don't we go down to the creek," Jasmine suggested. "We can warm up and have something to eat. If Blue-Scar is following us, he'd never think of looking down there." And we won't have to cross the bridge, she added to herself. At least not for a while.

They half-scrambled, half-slid down the slope. At the bottom they found a rock outcrop, sheltered from the wind. They built a fire for the kettle and rice pot, and were warming their hands when they heard a rustling sound. They looked around, but could see nothing. The rustling continued, punctuated now and then with coughs and moans. "There's someone in there," Jasmine said. "In that cluster of trees."

They crept toward a clearing in the alders and found an old man kneeling in front of a ragged tent, trying to start a fire. "Come and share our food," Keung said. "We have a fire close to the creek."

The man started at the sound of Keung's voice. With great difficulty he straightened, leaning on a stick for support. He turned toward them slowly, as if the slightest movement caused pain.

Jasmine gasped at the sight of his face. It was horribly swollen and discoloured with bruises. His feet and legs were swollen too, and he moaned with each rasping breath.

Keung stared, frozen with shock.

The man shook, as if overcome by a sudden chill. "Scurvy," he said hoarsely. "First the feet swell. Then the legs. And the eyes. When the shaking becomes too violent, you know there is not much time left." He gave a weak smile as if shrugging off the inevitable, and forced himself to stand taller, in a gesture of defiance.

Keung struggled to speak. It couldn't be. And yet — the tilt of the man's head, the shrug of the shoulders, the way he stood, even now, desperate to maintain his dignity. Finally, in a strangled cry, the word came out. "Father!"

Chapter 18

Chan Sam took a step, dazed and unbelieving. "Keung? How can this be?" Overcome by another bout of shaking, he collapsed in his son's arms.

Keung and Jasmine half-carried him to their shelter and propped him up by the fire. Keung prepared a cup of tea, added special herbs, and handed it to his father.

"You found me just before I am to die," Chan Sam said weakly. "The gods have had some part in this. Or Bright Jade." He peered at Jasmine through swollen eyelids. "Although she is not what I expected."

"This is Jasmine, Father. She's from another time, but she's not Bright Jade."

Chan Sam shrugged. "It doesn't matter. She has led you to the tiger, after all."

"What about you, Father? What happened?"

In a faltering voice, struggling to control the shaking, he explained. "I was in Lytton. The white boss fired two men in my gang. Too lazy, he said. The bookman gave them another chance. But after two hours, they were fired again. The boss refused to pay them for the two hours. So we attacked the boss and three others with rocks and shovels and pick handles. It was wrong, but we were so angry. One man was badly hurt. The next night —" He hunched over, seized by a fit of coughing.

"The next night," he continued, "a group of whites attacked our camp. They set fire to our bunkhouse. When we ran out, they beat us." He ran a hand over his bruised face, wincing at the touch. "My friend died of the beating. Many were badly hurt. But the white doctors in Lytton would not treat us. We had to send for the Chinese doctor in Yale."

"I hope they were arrested," Jasmine said.

"Nothing happened," he said bitterly. "We identified the leaders, but they got off. After that, I left Lytton. I had to get to Victoria and find a way to return to China."

He paused, worn out by the effort of talking. "I became weaker and weaker. I was afraid the coolies would take my possessions and leave me if they saw I was ill. So I came down to this creek. In a dream I saw the white jade tiger coming to life in my hand. Growing larger and larger until it opened its jaws and devoured me, one piece at a time. I screamed and woke up, drenched with sweat. Shaking. I knew I didn't have much time. Now I know I can go no farther."

Keung gave an anguished cry. "Why did you never write? Three years without a word!"

Tears welled up in Chan Sam's eyes. "I was too ashamed. I'm sorry." His shoulders heaved with racking coughs. "I found the tiger in the mud. I should have reburied it, but I thought it would change our fortunes. I thought it would bring good luck."

In a halting voice, he asked, "Do you know about Blue-Scar Wong?"

Keung nodded. "He's been following us, hoping to find you and the white jade tiger. We left him behind at Hell's Gate."

"Wong took the tiger from me. I stole it back. Then I fled Victoria." His words were broken by violent shaking and another fit of coughing.

"Rest now, Father. Don't try to speak."

Chan Sam brushed him aside and continued, his voice lowered to a raspy whisper. "The whites tried to take it away when they attacked the camp. But every time they touched it, their fingers burned." He fumbled with the leather thong around his neck. "What a terrible weight. It grows heavier and heavier. Too long I have carried this curse. Take it." He handed Keung the priceless piece of jade.

Jasmine stared at the tiger, luminous as moonlight. Every muscle was finely etched in the stone. Strength, power and magic pulsed from within, as if the tiger might spring to life at any moment.

"You must take the tiger home," Chan Sam said. "Remember the prophecy. *Dreams turn to dust, until the white jade tiger sleeps again.* It grows restless. Unless it is returned, it will destroy —" He stopped, seized by another attack of shaking.

"We'll take you to Yale," Jasmine said. "There's a doctor there."

"Too late," he said. "Joss has it otherwise. The curse of the tiger has it otherwise. But listen, my son. I do not wish to remain here as a ghost. Promise to mark my grave and send my bones home to China."

"Yes, Father."

"And find a hiding place for the tiger. There are those who do not fear its curse." He drained the last of his tea and fell forward, face in hands, exhausted.

They carried him to his tent and tucked the frayed quilt around him. In no time, he was asleep.

"He is not yet fifty," said Keung. "And already he is an old, old man. This Gold Mountain is killing my people."

"It won't always be like this," Jasmine said. "In my time —"

"Please. Do not talk about your time. Living in my time is enough of a burden right now. I have found my father only to watch him die. It is too hard for you to understand."

"You're wrong. I do understand."

Long into the night she cried, for her loss and for his. And it seemed as though all the ghosts in the canyon cried with her.

Ghosts stirred the dreams of Chan Sam. They showed him the white jade tiger buried in the mud. And a hand, pulling it out. They showed him his greed and selfishness, taking the jade to Gold Mountain, ignoring the prophecy. They also showed him a strong, fearless image of himself, drilling holes into rock walls, carving roads out of the granite cliffs. *Ah yes,* he sighed in his sleep. They had moved mountains. But what of their dreams? What of their Gold Mountain?

"Aiee!" he cried, stretching out his arms to the wailing ghosts. "I remember you — crushed to death by a rolling log. And you — drowned when you fell from the unfinished bridge. And you — who are you? You, without a head?" He screamed in horror.

Keung rushed to his side. "Father, wake up. It's only a dream."

"No," he gasped. "It's not a dream. We were not given a proper warning and my friend — his head was blown off in an explosion." He sobbed with despair. "These ghosts will not rest until they are given a proper burial. But how will we find their bones?" He grabbed Keung's arm. "Do you remember the Great Wall of China? And the tomb of Bright Jade's Emperor? Stone by stone we built that wall and died for someone's dream. Year after year we dug into the earth, building a kingdom for the Emperor, dying for his dream. And this railway! Here we are in a foreign land, breaking our backs and our hearts for someone else's dream. But what of *our* dreams? What of yours?"

The ghosts did not disturb Keung's dream, that night by Skuzzy Creek. He dreamed of a girl, dressed in the clothes of a coolie. She was swinging over a river, her long dark hair trailing like the feathery branches of bamboo. As he watched, she let go of the rope and plunged into the water. Frantically, he waited for her to come up. But when she emerged it was not from the river.

She stepped out of Fan Tan Alley, her face bright with laughter. He followed her along a street he did not recognize, a paved street, full of sounds and colours, lined with flowering cherry trees. At the end of the street was a gate, golden and splendid, with three roofs of glazed tiles curving up at the corners. Brightly painted panels shone in the sunlight — the phoenix and the dragon, green earth and blue sky, yin and yang.

The girl was passing through the gate, passing to the other side. Once she passed through, he knew he would never see her again. Desperately, he called her name, "Jasmine, wait! Don't go!" But she did not hear him. She did not see him. He had become a ghost.

In Jasmine's dream a parcel arrived from her father. When she opened it she found a pair of red satin slippers, embroidered with tigers in silk threads of blue, white, and gold. When she put them on, the tigers roared to life, leaped off the slippers and vanished.

She awoke expecting to be back in Fan Tan Alley. After all, they had found Keung's father and the white jade tiger. Instead, she woke to a brilliant sunrise over the Fraser Canyon. The ground glittered with frost.

She shivered and wrapped the quilt more tightly around her. From the far side of the trestle came the sounds of hammers and picks as coolies began their day's work. And from the cluster of alders came another sound.

She rose to find Keung piling rocks on top of a freshly dug grave, his face taut with unshed tears. She stood beside him in silence, clasping his hand. There was nothing to say.

"I'll find work in Victoria," Keung said as they climbed the slope to the tracks. "As a servant, maybe. Or as a woodcutter or vegetable peddler."

"Don't forget the merchant we met on the sternwheeler."

"Oh, yes, Lam Fu Choy. I had forgotten." He paused for a moment. "You will go back to your time?"

"I guess so." She had been puzzling over that very thought. How would it happen? The last time, Bright Jade had appeared in a dream. Jasmine had followed her somehow, and woken up in Fan Tan Alley. Maybe she had to be asleep to get back. Maybe she had to be in Chinatown.

They walked quickly, anxious to reach Yale and take the sternwheeler back to Victoria. Every so often Jasmine saw Keung touching the tiger, as if to make certain it was still there. "Where will you hide it?" she wondered.

"I'll ask Dragon Maker to hide it in one of his dragons."

"Won't Blue-Scar Wong look there, like he did before?"

"I'll say my father died before I could find him. I'll say he's buried somewhere near Lytton, along with the tiger."

Somehow, she didn't think it would be that simple.

The last rays of sunlight were sinking into the river as they passed Hell's Gate. The mouth of yet another tunnel loomed ahead. Jasmine shuddered. Tunnels were bad enough in the daylight, let alone after dark. "Let's camp here," she said. "I'm ready for something to eat."

They bustled about in an easy silence, building the fire and preparing the meal. It occurred to her that they were good at this, that in their short time together they had developed a comfortable routine. The thought made her smile. "You know," she said, "this will probably be our last night in the canyon." Something shifted inside as she spoke, a rush of sadness or regret so sharp it startled her. She realized that she didn't want to leave him. Didn't want to go back. And yet …

His voice, soft and urgent, pushed into her thoughts. "Do you hear something?"

She strained to listen. A low bubbling of water, the whish of steam, the crackling of flames. She shook her head and reached for more tea. Keung put out his hand to stop her. "Listen." He stared into the darkness beyond the fire.

The rustling of leaves on a windless night. The padding of footsteps. "Someone's coming," Jasmine whispered. A thrill of fear brushed her spine. She caught a glint of steel. And knew who it was.

Chapter 19

Jasmine felt a sickening lurch in her stomach as the figure stepped into the firelight. She swallowed hard. "Blue-Scar Wong," she said. She tried to keep her voice from quivering. "Are you afraid of tigers in the night?" Her eyes flashed to the knife in his hand.

Blue-Scar Wong flicked the blade with his thin fingers. His face was a crumpled mask of papier-mâché, twisted and grotesque. He gave a malicious smile and the scar gleamed lurid blue in the firelight. "Tigers?" he hissed. "It is not a fear of tigers that led me to you, but a desire to take back what is mine. Give me the white jade."

"We don't have it," Keung said.

Blue-Scar scowled. "I saw your father hand it to you. I heard his words. I care nothing for the curse of this white jade tiger. That does not affect me. What affects me is its value. Selling it will make me a very rich man. Besides, your father stole it from me and I want it back."

"It belonged to my father," Keung said heatedly. "The bailiff had no right to take it from him or to sell it. If you hadn't lied, it would have been returned to him long ago."

"You should be happy I'm taking it off your hands," Blue-Scar said. "The white jade tiger has brought nothing but grief to your family. How many dead now? Three sisters, your brother, your father, not to mention all the others in your clan. When I take it, you'll have a better chance of staying alive."

"That's not how it works," Jasmine said sharply. "No matter who has it, Keung's family suffers. Until the tiger returns to Bright Jade's grave."

"Who are you to know so much about the white jade tiger?" He spun around, his words hitting her like blows. "You, a pitiful coolie, cowering in my gambling den, scrabbling along the tracks. But perhaps you are not what you seem. Who are you? And what business is this of yours?" His eyes pierced hers.

Jasmine remained silent. Fear gnawed at her belly, her heart pounded in her ears, but she met his stare without flinching.

Finally he blinked and looked away. "Bah!" he spat. "You've been hearing too many stories, too many legends of the past. Forget them. You are here now, to stay. Both of you. You will never return to

China. I, on the other hand, may go back with my riches after selling the jade." His voice turned ugly and hard. "Give it to me."

"I *will* return to China," Keung retorted. "And when I go, the tiger will come with me." His hand edged toward the fire. He flashed a look at Jasmine, his eyes darting from Blue-Scar to the fire, then back again. Be ready, they said.

"You are an ignorant, worthless boy," Blue-Scar growled, pointing his knife at Keung. "If you don't hand over the tiger —"

He never had time to finish. In a sudden move, Keung lifted the kettle and pitched it straight at him. The kettle smashed against the side of his head and the scalding water spilled over his face. "Aieeee!" he screamed.

Keung and Jasmine sped toward the tunnel.

"I'll kill you!" The words blasted through the canyon as Blue-Scar Wong shot after them, livid with rage.

"Run, Jasmine! Run!" Keung cried.

Another voice urged her on. The dream voice, louder and clearer than ever. *Jasmine, run! Don't look back!* She felt tiger slippers on her feet, felt the tigers awakening, rushing her on at a dizzying speed.

Taking courage from the tigers she flew through the night. She could hear her heartbeat drumming along the tracks. She could hear Keung, close behind. She could hear Blue-Scar Wong heaving behind them, closer and closer —

Don't look back! Too late. Glancing over her shoulder she caught the flash of steel whizzing through the air, felt her knees buckle and slam against the rail, and felt her head smash on the wooden tie.

When she opened her eyes the sky had gone. There were no stars, no moon. Only darkness. Panic rose in a knot, squeezing her stomach, strangling her throat so she couldn't swallow. Had she been buried alive? No, rain was falling on her face. No, not rain. Water, dripping from the roof and down the rock walls. She was in the tunnel.

Come on. Get up. She stumbled toward the sound of scuffling and voices.

"Where is it?" Blue-Scar had Keung against the wall of the tunnel, the tip of the knife at his throat.

"No," Keung gasped. Blue-Scar pressed the knife deeper into the skin. "My … my bag."

Blue-Scar struck him across the face. "I've torn apart your bag. You know it's not there. Where is it?" The knife broke the skin. Keung felt something wet trickle down his neck and knew it was blood.

With a shudder he closed his eyes, silently asking his father and all his ancestors to forgive him. The image of Bright Jade flashed through his mind but disappeared as Blue-Scar hit him again. Gasping for breath, he struggled with the words. "Inside my …"

"NO!" Jasmine's movement was so sudden Blue-Scar didn't know what hit him. All he could see was a blur that leaped from the blackness of the tunnel and knocked him to the ground. A figure loomed over him, arms raised, legs bent, poised, ready to strike. As he started to rise, it kicked him in the throat and sent him sprawling. He felt the second kick coming, grabbed the leg and gave it a vicious twist. Jasmine shrieked and fell onto the tracks as Blue-Scar grappled for her throat.

"I told you not to interfere!" he shouted.

Fighting for breath, she raked her fingers through his scalded face until he let go, howling with pain. She seized her chance. Rolled out of his way and staggered to her feet, desperate to get out of the tunnel. At the same time she heard Keung screaming, "TRAIN!"

With a rising sense of horror, she felt it. The thundering rumble, the vibrations of the track. How far away was it? The beam from the headlight was hazy, but growing sharper and brighter. From the corner of her eye she saw Keung fumbling in his jacket. "Leave it!" she cried. "Run!"

Before she could move she was pinned by the headlight, as piercing as the eye of a tiger. She froze. Heard the whistle. Saw the burst of white steam.

Blue-Scar lunged toward her. She darted to one side, and hurled herself at him with all her strength. Caught him off balance, pushed him onto the tracks. Flattened herself against the wall. As a white shape roared through the tunnel, growing in size until it consumed the darkness, its body fierce and terrible.

Finally the thundering stopped and the ground stopped shaking. In the distance Jasmine heard the mournful whistle of the train. She felt a movement beside her, and reached over to clasp Keung's hand. In horrified silence they stared at the mangled heap in the centre of the tracks.

"It was the train," Keung gasped. "He fell into the path of the train."

Jasmine took shallow breaths to quiet the sound of her breathing. "No. I pushed him. I mean … there was something else. Didn't you see it? The white shape, just before the train …"

Her leg hurt, her chest hurt, and her head felt ready to explode. *If I could get out of the tunnel,* she thought. *Away from this.* She sank to the ground, shaking with the horror of what lay on the tracks. *If I could get to the daylight….* She buried her face in her arms. Daylight was still a long time away.

As she was falling asleep she thought she heard Keung's stunned cry and the words, "The tiger is gone."

Sleep was comforting. For a long time the darkness was shut out and there were no dreams to disturb her. But little by little, consciousness stole in. She shivered and reached for the quilt, but it wasn't there. When she opened her eyes to search for it, she was surprised to see a light in the tunnel, beckoning like a candle flame. She rose and slipped toward it. But as she approached, it grew smaller and smaller, until its brightness was concentrated in one form — a white jade tiger lying in the centre of the tracks, beside the broken remains of Blue-Scar Wong. Shuddering, she picked up the tiger and crept toward Keung. She placed it in his open palm, smiling as he sighed in his sleep and closed his hand around it.

Another light shimmered at the end of the tunnel. She moved toward it, unaware of the darkness, unaware of her footsteps on the tracks. The light was growing, changing, shining with greater intensity. As she stepped out of the tunnel it shifted into a familiar shape, warm and welcoming. Luminous, like Bright Jade.

The spirit floated off the tracks, down the slope toward the river. "Wait!" Jasmine cried. "I can't keep up with you." The spirit turned to her and smiled with the face of her mother. And in her mother's voice whispered, "The time has not yet come, Dragon Girl."

Frantically Jasmine clambered down the slope. "Stop!"

She reached out her arms, trying to catch hold of the fleeing shape. Suddenly, she stumbled. Her injured leg buckled beneath her. The next instant she was caught up in a tumble of stones, sliding down to the river below.

Chapter 20

"Oh god," Jasmine groaned. Pain throbbed through her head, into the backs of her eyes, along every nerve in her body. Every muscle ached. Slowly, tentatively, she stretched out hands, arms, legs, testing to make sure nothing was broken.

"Are you all right?" a voice asked. She glanced up to see a young Chinese woman, her face creased with concern. "We heard a loud clattering. You must have fallen down the stairs."

Stairs? No, she had fallen down the riverbank. But … that wasn't right. Where was the river? She looked around, dazed. A staircase, backs of buildings, cement walkways. People in modern clothing. Traffic sounds, a radio blaring through an open window. Was she back in Chinatown? Could this be the courtyard off Fan Tan Alley, where Dragon Maker lived? It wasn't possible.

And it was so cold. A raw cold that stung the back of her throat. How could it be so cold in —

Wait. It wasn't September. She was back, and it was February. Where was Keung? She had left him sleeping in the tunnel. Was he still there? "I've got to go back," she muttered. "I have to —"

"You shouldn't be here, you know," the woman said. "There's a gate across the passageway in the alley."

"I know," Jasmine said. "Hell's Gate."

The woman gave her a puzzled look. "Are you sure you're all right? Here, let me help you." Jasmine took her arm and stood up shakily. She took small steps, fighting the dizziness, struggling to regain a sense of control.

"There's Fan Tan Alley," the woman said as they reached the gate. "Fisgard's to the left. You're sure you're okay? I could phone someone."

"I'm … I'm fine. Thank you." A voice whirred inside her head. This is how it ends? What about Keung? What about seeing it through? Suddenly, she remembered her backpack. She had left it at Dragon Maker's to be less conspicuous. "Do you know about Dragon Maker?" she asked. "The old man who used to hide things in his dragons?"

The woman smiled, surprised. "My grandparents used to tell me that story!"

"I found one of the dragons," Jasmine said. "And I met Dragon Maker."

"It's just a story," the woman said. She unlocked the gate and gave Jasmine a pat on the shoulder. "Go home," she said. "Take a rest from dragons."

Somehow, her footsteps led her down Fisgard, along Store Street and onto the Johnson Street Bridge. It was too brash and glaring, the roar of traffic, the bustle of people. Lights shone green, red, and amber. Words flashed: Walk, Don't Walk. *Run*. Her heart raced, her knees trembled. Stop. Go. No tunnels. No river. No tiger. Her feet moved reluctantly, unsure of this strange new world. *But this is your world,* she reminded herself. *And your time*. Still, she could not make a connection.

Curious stares followed her, marking her as the stranger she felt herself to be. She tried to shrug them off, but the feeling of disorientation clung to her as closely as the well-worn jacket. She paused on the bridge and looked over the harbour, longing to see the wharves and the sternwheelers, longing to see Keung. But the magic was gone and the harbour did not change.

The voice in her head kept whirring. *Maybe if you go back. If you go back to the never-ending store and through the door again. Turn around and go back. Now!*

But her footsteps outpaced the voice. Before she knew it she was at her aunt's. And it was too late to go back.

"Jasmine!" Val exclaimed. "Back so soon? I wasn't expecting you for an hour or so. Did you get the tea? Let's have some now."

Jasmine crumpled at the kitchen table. Tea? She'd completely forgotten. And an hour? She glanced at her wrist and remembered she'd left her watch at Dragon Maker's along with everything else. The kitchen clock showed 10:15. It would have taken about ten minutes to walk home and she'd gone into the store right at 10:00. All that time with Keung, all that time in the canyon was … nothing.

Val sat down, studying her niece. "Are you feeling okay? You look like you've been through the wringer. What happened to your clothes? And your face? You haven't been hurt, have you?"

It was too much. Jasmine lowered her head and sobbed. "I forgot everything! The tea and the postcard, and I left the dragon and the old coin with Dragon Maker and I don't know if Keung got back to Victoria …"

"Suppose you tell me what happened," Val said, hugging her. "I'll put the kettle on."

The minutes ticked away. Through questions and answers and tears. As the time passed — *Was it really passing?* Jasmine wondered, looking at the clock. *Here it's passing, but somewhere else, in another time, it's not. It's stopped, completely.* As the time passed, she felt lighter, relieved in the telling, as if a bamboo pole had been lifted from her shoulders.

"It started with Bright Jade, didn't it?"

Jasmine stared at her aunt, astounded. How could she have known?

"Your mother used to dream about Bright Jade," Val explained. "And the white jade tiger. She used to keep me awake, talking about it, trying to get it out of her mind. She had nightmares, too."

"When did they start? Did they last for a long time?"

"They started just after our mother died. And they stopped suddenly, right about the time Heather tore off the coolie clothes, the ones you're wearing. She never mentioned the dreams again. You know," Val said, "I was jealous of Heather. I kept wondering why I couldn't have the dreams. I thought they were some kind of message. I kept going to Chinatown, trying to find the answer. Heather thought I was crazy."

"Didn't she like going to Chinatown?"

Val shook her head. "That's why the dreams bothered her so much. She was like our parents. They didn't want to acknowledge our Chinese connection either. Our grandparents had distanced themselves from it and our parents didn't want to be reminded of it. Your mom felt the same way."

"What do you mean? What Chinese connection?"

Val's blue eyes widened. "You mean you don't know? Heather never told you? Your great-great-grandfather was Chinese!"

Spirits wove through her dream like fireflies, one light shimmering to the next. Nearest and brightest was her mother. And farthest away was Bright Jade.

Jasmine woke up, turned on the lamp, and studied her face in the mirror. She didn't look Chinese. But in the coolie clothes, she hadn't looked white. She was one, she was the other. She was both. Dragon Maker had known. And a part of her must have known. Otherwise, how could she have fitted in? How could the magic have worked, if not for that part of her?

And why had her mother kept it a secret?

"You have to imagine the scandal at the time," Val had said. "A Chinese man married to a white woman? His family would have been as outraged as hers. They must have been very brave, and very much in love, to go through with it. And the Chinese were treated so badly in those days. Maybe that's why their children wanted to forget."

"Why didn't Mom tell me?"

"Maybe she didn't think it was important. A lot of people focus on the present and don't think too much about the past."

"That's why your parents didn't like you going to Chinatown?"

"They thought it best to leave well enough alone, and not venture into the past at all."

Jasmine curled up on the window seat and gazed at the city lights. She thought of Keung, arriving long ago, young and alone. All those lives, coming in, going out, like the campfires flickering through the canyon. Did he go back to China? Did he take the white jade tiger home?

She missed him. She wanted to say, *Guess what! I learned something about my ancestors. My great-great-grandfather was Chinese. Do you think he knows I travelled into the past and spoke his language? Is he proud of me, do you think?*

A few days later, the parcel arrived. "The slippers," Jasmine exclaimed, tearing off the brown paper. "I had a dream about them."

Sure enough, there were the slippers, embroidered with the heads of tigers. Tucked inside was a letter.

Dear Jasmine, I really miss you and lasagna — in that order. Actually, I'm enjoying the food and learning the tricks of wokerie. You're in for some delicious treats.

Jasmine groaned. "Oh no. He's going to get carried away again." *I've got a week's holiday in April and hope you will join me for some exploring. A fellow teacher has talked me into visiting her relatives in Guangdong, a province in the south. So how about it? Most of the Chinese who worked on the CPR came from that part of China.*

"Does he know about our Chinese connection?" Jasmine asked.

"I never thought so," Val said, "but I could be wrong. I know that Guangdong is where my great-grandfather came from."

Jasmine read on. *I've booked you a flight in April. You'll love it — sorry, let me rephrase that to: I'm sure you might possibly have an interesting time.*

"I hate it when he tells me I'll love something," Jasmine explained. "Like when he told me I'd love staying with you. I got furious."

"Is it that bad?"

"No," she said. "I love it!"

About the slippers. The Chinese believe the tiger is the king of beasts, not the lion. He's as important as the dragon. The Blue Dragon was said to rule over the east and the White Tiger ruled over the west. Demons were supposed to be terrified of the tiger, so it was painted on walls of houses and temples to scare away evil spirits, and embroidered on children's shoes for the same reason. I suspect you could scare away evil spirits without any help from the tigers, but I thought you might like them all the same. And remember, the longest journey starts with a single step, whether you're wearing tiger shoes or not. So I hope to see you soon. A longer letter will follow, with more words of wisdom, etc. All my love, Dad.

P.S. They say a tiger lives to be 1,000 years old, and when he's 500 his colour changes to white. His claws are a powerful good luck charm, if you ever happen to come across any. So keep that in mind, okay?

In no time at all, it was April.

"You're really going to China? On Monday? When we're suffering in school? You're so lucky!"

"Yes!" said Jasmine. She was waiting for Val, surrounded by her teacher and classmates. Her bag was loaded with cards and scraps of paper with everyone's address, and her mind was stuffed with instructions. "Don't worry. I'll send post-cards of the Great Wall and the terracotta warriors and I'll bring back pictures of rice paddies and dragons, and I won't forget that Krista wants a bell for her bike."

"And I'd like a jade carving," said Mrs. Butler.

"Dream on!" Jasmine said with a grin.

"When will you be back?" Krista asked.

"In time for the summer holidays. Too late for strawberries, but we'll plant the garden like we planned last year, okay?"

"Great! With a pagoda, maybe?"

Jasmine laughed. "Sure, why not? My aunt's here now, I've got to go."

"Don't forget us. Keep up the tai chi. See you!"

Then she was gone.

Saturday morning. Everything was organized, packed, checked, and double-checked. There was nothing to do but wait, except for one thing. She had to go back. Just one more time.

She took the coolie clothes from the closet and put them on. Braided her hair into one long queue. Placed the hat on her head.

Val gave her a worried look. "You're obviously heading for Chinatown. Are you sure that's a good idea?"

Jasmine nodded. "I'll be back when I'm back."

Chapter 21

Don't get your hopes up, she told herself as she dashed across the bridge. *It might not work. The key might be in the dragon or in the coin, remember? Neither of which you have. So don't get your hopes up.*

But she carried on regardless, fired up with the certainty that it would work. Because it had to. It couldn't end with so many missing pieces.

Into the never-ending store, through the connecting rooms, and into the back. So far, everything was the same. "Can I go out this way?" she asked, pointing to the *No Exit* sign on the door.

"Sure," said the clerk.

Through the doorway — and into the Fan Tan Alley of another time. It worked! Not only that, she had the good fortune to step right into the midst of Chinese New Year celebrations.

The clanging and clamouring left no mistake. She could hear the clashing of cymbals and pounding of drums, the excited shrieks of people, the bursting of fireworks. Her stomach fluttered with excitement and she hugged herself with joy. Chinese New Year! Talk about auspicious. He was bound to be here.

Fisgard Street was ablaze with light and colour. Paper lanterns hung from every lamppost. Shops were decorated with peach sprays and red paper, printed with good luck verses. Long strands of firecrackers exploded, littering the ground with blossom-like drifts of red paper.

The street was crowded with people. Wealthy merchants in satin gowns glided from door to door. Ordinary workers greeted each other, bowing and shaking hands. Chinese women bustled past. Young children skipped by, eagerly clutching the *lai see* envelopes given to them by their elders. Chinatown was bright with smiles.

And white people! Jasmine had never seen so many, not in this place or time. She noticed new buildings too, three-storeys high, with fancy brickwork along the top and on the front. Arched windows and doorways opened onto iron balconies, decorated with scrolls proclaiming prosperity, long life, and good fortune.

She breathed in deeply, savouring the delicious smells that filtered through open doorways — nuts, pastries, fruits, delicacies saved for the New Year.

Wisps of smoke rose from burning joss sticks, filling the air with the scent of musk and sandalwood. She took another deep breath and smiled, thinking, *How wonderful to be here, to be back.*

As she darted through the crowds, searching for that one familiar face, a window display of *lai see* envelopes caught her eye. She stopped for a closer look and saw that each envelope was engraved with the gold figure of a tiger. The Year of the Tiger! So that would make it, what? She knew the Chinese zodiac had a cycle of twelve years. Keung was sixteen, born in the Year of the Tiger. One Tiger Year had passed, so now, in his second Tiger Year he would be —

She felt cold suddenly, and strangely unbalanced, as if something inside her had shifted. It couldn't be. And yet there was no mistaking the tiger. But Keung, twenty-four? A grown man? And the year would be — she did a quick calculation — 1890? Impossible! "Excuse me," she said, approaching a merchant. "Could you tell me what year it is?"

He walked by without a glance.

"Excuse me." She tried again. And again. And was struck with the horrifying realization that no one could see her. She had become the invisible stranger.

She leaned against a building and clawed at her braid, listening to her inner voice: *Don't get discouraged. Keep looking, you're sure to recognize him.*

If he's here. If he's not back in China.

But he *has* to be here. He's probably right on this street, waiting for the Lion Dance like everyone else.

But he'll be so old now. He won't remember you. Even if you do see him, which you probably —

Stop it! She chided herself as a cheer erupted, signalling the appearance of the lion dancers.

There were two dancers, one man in front, one behind, with a length of silk rippling in between. Leading the lion was the monk, his face hidden under a grinning mask of papier-mâché. He teased the lion, darting round the sinuous shape, while musicians pounded their drums and beat gongs and cymbals. The lion tossed his gigantic head and flashed his eyes, kicked out his feet, leaped, and jumped in wild, acrobatic movements, bounded into the crowd and back again to leap at the monk.

Moved by a sudden impulse, Jasmine stepped into the middle of the street and began to dance alongside the lion. Why not? No one could see her. Weaving in and out amongst the dancers, she searched the spectators for —

There, across the street. He was watching the Lion Dance, his eyes shining with excitement. Eagerly, she ran toward him.

Just then he turned and said something to the young woman beside him. They laughed as he bent down and picked up a small child. Jasmine froze. The woman was not Chinese. She was white. The child had dark hair and a light tan complexion. His eyes were huge with wonder, captivated by the antics of the lion. When he smiled, his face lit up like Keung's.

Jasmine ached with confusion. Could it really be him? No. The man was wearing Western clothes, not the clothes of a coolie. And his hair was short. Keung would not have cut his queue. And he was so much older. But of course he would be. Another Year of the Tiger — of course he would have lines on his face, of course his slight body would have filled out. And something else. He looked so confident and prosperous. So happy! And the little boy and the woman — were they a family?

The child said something and pointed to the dancing lion. With a flash of dimples, the man smiled and nodded. *Oh yes!* Jasmine's heart lurched with recognition. There was no mistake. She reached out and gently touched his shoulder. "Keung," she said. "I've come back."

He shifted the child in his arms and turned to the woman, waving his free hand as if dispelling a mist. The movement passed right through Jasmine, chilling her heart so that its beat became a small, faint quiver. He could no longer see her. But what did it mean? That he no longer believed? Had he turned his back on Bright Jade and the white jade tiger?

Once he turned in her direction. *He must feel my presence,* she thought. *He knows that I'm here.* She stepped closer and opened her mouth to speak. But he turned away. And her hopes were shattered, as surely as a china dragon smashed on stone.

As the dancers moved down the street, the crowd began to disperse. Chattering groups of people left for homes and restaurants. Keung and his family were swept along with the rest. Helplessly, Jasmine stood and watched them go, tears streaming down her face. Was this it? Was this the end? An aching sadness welled up inside. She wished she had never come back.

Somehow, she found herself in a courtyard behind Fisgard Street, standing at the top of a staircase before a freshly painted door.

"Come in, Jasmine." Dragon Maker clasped his hands and bowed as she entered. "I knew you would return."

"I waited too long," she said, choking back the tears. "I lost him. He couldn't — But it can't be 1890! It just can't!"

"It is indeed the Year of the Tiger, but that one has long passed. We are in a new century now, 1902." He smiled. "Time is no time at all, is it?"

"1902?" She stared at him, stunned. *Twenty* years had passed! A whole generation! No wonder everything had changed.

But not in this room. She looked at the bits and pieces of dragons, the pots of glaze and brushes still cluttering the shelves and table. "Did you hide the tiger for him? He said he would go back to China. He said he would return it to Bright Jade's grave."

"Joss had it otherwise. Keung never went back to China. He stayed in Victoria to work for Lam Fu Choy, the merchant. Once the railway was finished, the coolies were forced to fend for themselves. Many survived by begging, stealing, and picking through garbage. Keung has been lucky. He is clever and resourceful, a hard worker. Of course, his luck may change. But for now, he has prospered."

Dragon Maker lit his pipe. "For a long time, he waited for you to return. Then a letter came from his village saying his mother had died. Why hurry back? he thought. Why not stay here for a while? He stayed and waited for you. He sent his father's bones home to be buried, but he stayed and waited. After a time you became a memory, a dream. Another Bright Jade. So Keung embraced the Land of Gold Mountain and began a new life."

"But the white jade tiger? What about the curse on his family?"

"He turned his back on the prophecy. And so the curse follows him, and his children, and his children's children. Until the tiger sleeps again." He rose shakily and searched through a crate overflowing with dragons. Finally he found what he was looking for.

"You've come back for this," he said, handing her the backpack. "Keung wanted to take it. But I knew you would return to the Dragon Maker, sooner or later."

Jasmine rummaged through the pack. There was her watch and the *lai see* envelope with the 1881 coin inside. And there was the dragon. "Did you make this?" she asked.

Dragon Maker ran his hands over the blue-glazed dragon. "This was the first," he said. "The most special."

"Did you put a surprise in it?"

His eyes twinkled. "The dragon has the tiger, but not in the way you think. Now, if you'll excuse me, I'm going to indulge an old man's appetite in a New Year's Feast."

"No! You can't go yet! What about the little boy and that woman? I want to know — I still don't understand …"

He faced her from the doorway, framed by the good luck scrolls and faded Door Guardians. "Time passes, Sweet Jasmine," he said, smiling sadly. "Two years or two thousand, it passes. You cannot change what is written. You cannot change what has passed. If you do, then you erase yourself. Keung has turned his back on his past and faces a new future. And you face a future, returning to your past." Softly, he patted her cheek. "Thank you for coming. I will not see you again, but you have brightened many dreams." He turned and disappeared down the stairs.

"Wait!" Jasmine called. Grabbing her backpack, she ran after his frail figure as it slipped beneath lines of laundry and between ragged railings. "Wait! Do you mean I'm a dream? Am I real or aren't I? Was it all just a dream? Wait!" She stumbled over a loose brick. As she tried to stop the fall, the dragon slipped out of her backpack. The next thing she knew, she was sprawled out in Fan Tan Alley, surrounded by china fragments of bright, shattered blue.

Chapter 22

"So there was nothing in your dragon? Nothing at all?"

"Just this." Jasmine handed Val a small sachet filled with the fragrant petals of jasmine. "Some surprise."

"But it's *you*, don't you see? He always knew you'd come."

"I was hoping to find the white jade tiger." She shrugged aside her disappointment and retreated to the spare room to finish the quilt. All she needed was a few more dark pieces to match up with the remaining light ones. Then it would be done.

She picked through the scraps of fabric. Yellow, peach, turquoise.... Nothing dark. What she needed was a deep shadowy blue. Like the coolie jacket.

Why not? It was perfect for her memory quilt. And she wouldn't have to cut it all up, just a square, where it wouldn't show, so she'd still be able to wear it if she wanted to.

She spread out the jacket, trying to decide where to cut. There. The lining at the back, right beneath the shoulder.

She cut out a square, careful not to disturb the cotton padding underneath. As she was removing it, she felt a bump. *A lump of cotton*, she thought. *It got wadded up somehow, maybe when I washed it. Wait a minute….*

Her fingers pressed harder. No question about it, there was something inside. Something small and hard.

She cut into the padding. And there, buried inside, was a red ribbon wrapped round and round.

Sunrise flooded the canyon. Below the tracks the river roared in its rush to the sea. A boy sat at the edge of the tracks, hunched over a dark blue cotton jacket. With painstaking care he made the tiny stitches, so that no one would know what lay between the layers. The white jade tiger would be safe there, until it was time to go home.

Soon Jasmine would be back. She would be surprised when he showed her his hiding place, and pleased that he had wrapped her good luck ribbon around it.

The jagged cry of a bird made him look up. Just in time to see a mist rise above the river, swirl in a cloud of silk, and disappear in the morning sun.

Jasmine embraced the tiger as the vision faded. Now she understood. *It's you*, her aunt had said. And Dragon Maker's words — *the dragon has the tiger, but not in the way you think.*

She sewed the last square onto the quilt and stepped back to admire her work. The patterns shifted and changed, depending on how she looked at it. But the memories were there, light and dark, coming together to form a whole.

She ran her fingers over the dark-blue cotton and smiled. Bright Jade's spirit could rest now. The Dragon Girl was taking the tiger home.

Selected Chronology

1858

~The first Chinese arrive in Victoria from San Francisco

1873

~Anti-Chinese Society formed in Victoria

1878

~Bill passed to exclude Chinese from public works

~Bill passed which requires Chinese to buy a licence to stay, leading to a general strike of Chinese in Victoria

1879

~Andrew Onderdonk purchases contracts to construct the Canadian Pacific Railway through the Fraser Canyon

1880

~Construction of the railway begins in April; Chinese labourers arrive from Hong Kong in July

1881

~Chinese labourers arrive in larger numbers

1882

~Peak of Chinese immigration reached — 8,083 from San Francisco and Hong Kong

~September 28 — Chinese labourers pull the *Skuzzy* through Hell's Gate

1883

~Winter of 1882–83 — scurvy widespread amongst Chinese railway workers

~May 10, Lytton — Chinese killed in riot at CPR construction site

1884

~Unemployment and starvation amongst Chinese as railway construction slows down

1885

~Head Tax set at $50 for every Chinese entering Canada

~November 7 — the last spike is driven at Craigellachie, joining the west and east portions of the CPR

1887

~First train arrives in Vancouver

1901

~Head Tax on Chinese increased to $100

1904

~Head Tax increased to $500

1908

~Importation, manufacture, and sale of opium are prohibited by the Government of Canada

1923

~Exclusion Act: Chinese can no longer enter Canada

1947

~Chinese wives and unmarried children are allowed to enter Canada

1949

~Chinese in B.C. are given the right to vote

1967

~Chinese immigration is placed on an equal basis with other nationalities

Acknowledgements

The British Columbia Provincial Archives was an important source in the research of this book. The daily press of the times was immensely helpful, particularly the *Yale Sentinel*, the *Colonist*, and the *Mainland Guardian*. Other invaluable sources include *In a Sea of Sterile Mountains: The Chinese in British Columbia* by James Morton, *The Last Spike* by Pierre Berton, and David Chuenyan Lai's books: *Chinatowns: Towns Within Cities in Canada* and *The Forbidden City within Victoria*. Bruce Mason of the Yale and District Historical Society was extremely helpful in providing information on Yale in the early 1880s. A.C. Milliken's article *Early Sternwheelers on the Fraser River* (Hope Standard, 1956–57) provided more useful information.

I owe a debt of thanks to Dr. Daniel Bryant of the Pacific and Asian Studies Department, University of Victoria, for his help concerning the Chinese language, and to Gail Bryant, who read the manuscript and offered many helpful comments. Many thanks to Eng K. Ching for his invaluable comments, and to Paddy Tsurumi of the Department of History, University of Victoria, who read an early version of the manuscript and encouraged me to carry on. My gratitude to the friends and colleagues who showed an interest in this project, especially to my husband, Patrick, for his endless patience and encouraging words.

And finally, a special thanks to my editor, Guy Chadsey, who kept my spirits up during the inevitable periods of frustration, and whose enthusiasm and encouragement helped me through the journey.

Cherry Blossom Baseball
Jennifer Maruno

*CCBC's Best Books for Kids & Teens (Spring 2016) —
Commended*

Michiko Minigawa's life is nothing but a bad game of baseball.
The Canadian government swung the bat once, knocking her
family away from a Vancouver home base to an old farmhouse
in the Kootenay Mountains. But when they move into town,
the government swings the bat again, announcing that all
Japanese must now move east of the Rockies or else go to Japan.

Now in Ontario, Michiko once again has to adjust to a
whole new kind of life. She is the only Japanese student in
her school, and making friends is harder than it was before.
When Michiko surprises an older student with her baseball
skills and he encourages her to try out for the local team, she
gives it a shot. But everyone thinks this new baseball star is a
boy. Michiko has to make a decision: quit playing ball (and
being harassed), or pitch like she's never pitched before.

Darkling Green
Kim Thompson

Spring comes to Eldritch Manor, bringing with it all kinds of mayhem. The arrival of the King of the Fairies throws the resident fairies into a romantic tizzy. Mab neglects her knitting, resulting in holes in time through which any manner of evil can enter their world. Nature, weather, and time itself are all out of whack, and everyone is freaked about Willa's upcoming "unlucky" thirteenth birthday. On top of everything, Willa makes a shocking discovery about her mother, which supports Belle's claim that Willa is part mermaid!

Willa is plagued with questions. How can she be a mermaid if she doesn't have a tail and is terrified of water? How long do dragons hibernate? Why are there time holes in the pool, and where do they lead? Why are the backyard plants invading the house? And why does she keep dreaming about a sinister Green Man?

Bone Deep
Gina McMurchy-Barber

An expedition to investigate an old sunken ship teaches Peggy lessons about herself.

When archaeologists discover a two-hundred-year-old shipwreck, Peggy Henderson decides she'll do whatever it takes to take part in the expedition. But first she needs to convince her mom to let her go, and to pay for scuba diving lessons. To complicate matters even more, Peggy's Great Aunt Beatrix comes to stay, and she's bent on changing Peggy from a twelve-year-old adventure-seeking tomboy to a proper young lady. Help comes in the most unlikely of places when Peggy gets her hands on a copy of the captain's log from the doomed ship, which holds the key to navigating stormy relationships.